CHANGING THE FUTURE

I0653128

DIANE WINTERS

First published in 2025 by Blossom Spring Publishing
Changing The Future © 2025 Diane Winters
ISBN 978-1-917938-22-8
E: admin@blossomspringpublishing.com
W: www.blossomspringpublishing.com

1

A bell chimed to alert Martine that someone had entered the shop. She took off her glasses, tucked her pencil into her messy bun, and stretched before getting out of her chair. She looked through the office window and saw a man standing in the entryway, neither moving forward nor looking around. He, more or less, seemed rooted to the spot. She walked into the shop and headed his way.

"May I help you with something today?"

The man appeared startled and jerked his head toward her. "Oh. Sorry. I'm looking for Charity. Is she here?"

"No. I'm sorry. She hasn't been here for over five years."

The man appeared dismayed as he stretched his hand out toward the merchandise. "All of these are her creations, right?"

"You are correct."

"I don't understand. The shop hasn't changed much since I was here last. You say she hasn't been here for five years?"

"Yes. That's right." Martine looked around. "I keep the place dusted and sell a piece now and then. Business is pretty slow in this neighborhood. The gentrification of our downtown area has pulled most of the shops out of the area. Lately, it's only the customers who are looking specifically for Charity's artwork that meander down here. Was there something of interest you were looking for?"

"I wanted to talk to Charity herself." The man looked at Martine and studied her features: her hair, pulled up on top of her head into a bun, looked as if it was threatening to explode at any moment. What caught him off guard were the black eyes peering out at him from under the long bangs. With all that blond hair he figured she would have blue or green eyes. He shook himself. "I'm sorry. My name is Xavier." He stretched out his hand.

"Martine." She shook his hand as she studied the stranger. Pleasant to look at, his dark features and his mannerisms made him seem quite mysterious. "I'm afraid I can't tell you how to get ahold of her. I'm renting the workshop from her, and in exchange for the loft apartment, I keep an eye on the shop."

"You must have to contact her for something, don't you?"

"Actually, in all the time I've been here, there has been no reason for me to try and reach her personally. I deposit the rent directly into her bank account. If something needs repaired, the bank gets the bill and they pay it for her. I assume they take care of everything. I certainly don't."

"What a strange situation."

Martine shrugged and looked around the shop. "Well, if there isn't anything else I can do for you, then I need to get back to work."

"Fine, fine." Xavier started for the door but turned back. "You mentioned using the workshop. What do you do?"

"Sculptures, but only on a contract basis. Nothing in

the shop is mine."

He looked around one more time. "I can see that."

He slowly turned and headed out the door, the bell tinkling again as he left the shop. Martine watched him walk to a fancy BMW and get in. The man sat and looked back at the shop for a few moments before he drove away. She walked to the front of the shop and looked out at the slow-moving traffic. Xavier was long gone, but the questions remained. Who was he, and why did he want to talk to Charity? She glanced at her watch and decided to lock up. The shop hours were only a few hours a day, anyway. With store traffic so rare these days, if someone really wanted to buy something, they could come back another time. Martine shook her head and started back to the office. Appreciating the break from bending over her desk sketching out her next project, she decided it was a good time to have a late lunch. Or maybe she should say an early supper. Whatever it was, Martine headed upstairs to the loft apartment. Living on the premises was great, but it also meant she would forget about the time and work long hours without breaks. And when she was in the middle of a project, she rarely left the building at all.

A little over five years ago, Martine had walked into Charity's Shoppe to discuss renting a portion of the building. She felt another artist would understand the need for a wide-open space and hoped to use a part of her workshop. A mutual friend mentioned that Charity had a large space in the back that was never used and encouraged Martine to discuss the possibility. Upon entering the shop, she was immediately overwhelmed by the art on display. Crystal, glass, and mirrored items filled the front of the shop, along with huge objects hanging from beams in the open ceiling. Everything provided a prism of color as the sun shone through the overly large front glass windows. Upper windows on two sides of the shop made the place so bright it wasn't even necessary to turn on the lights during a sunshiny day. Martine knew, as soon as she walked in, that it was no wonder Charity was highly successful.

Martine eventually got up the courage to explain why she was there. Charity was used to people being a little overwhelmed when they met her, so she was very gracious to the younger woman. Once Martine was finally escorted through the shop to the back, she was surprised. The place was huge, and Charity was only using a small part of the space. With a back entrance that Martine could use without disturbing Charity, they came to a verbal agreement. Surprised there wasn't more to it than that, she promised to be a great renter. Then one day, only a few months later, Charity offered her a proposition.

"I've appreciated your work ethic and the results of your hard work. I'm not sure if this is something you would consider, but I'm going to leave the area very soon and my place will be empty. Would you be interested in living in my apartment and running my shop?"

Martine's eyes popped wide open and she couldn't get her mouth to work. She spluttered, "Where are you going? I mean, I have my own projects that I must complete. I don't have time to run your shop all day."

Charity nodded. "I know. And I also realize you have no idea what is going on in this area of town. All the shops are pulling out, and there are only a few of us left. I'm not moving. Can you imagine the mess I'd have on my hands trying to crate and transport all my art without breakages? I have very little business now, and I don't care. I need to get away from it all. I'm tired. I have everything arranged at the bank, and if you don't want to move in, I will close down the shop and just leave it as is."

"Hmm. Give up my apartment and move in here? What if you wanted to come back? Then where would I live?"

"I promise that if I decide to come back, I'll give you plenty of time to find another apartment. Or I'll just get my own place. I've lived here for years and I'm ready for a change." She snapped her fingers. "Oh. And if you decide to live here, I won't charge you rent if you keep the shop open."

"But I still pay rent for the workspace."

"Nothing changes except that you will live and work out of the same space, just like I did. And if you ever want to close the shop and move out, feel free. I won't hold you here. If you get tired of the whole retail gig, feel free to hang a closed sign and shut the lights off. All I ask is you keep the place dusted occasionally. My concern is having someone break in if they finally figure out no one is here. That's why I would love for you to live in the loft, even if the store is closed."

"When do you need to know?"

"By next week. I'm packing up my belongings as we speak and finalizing my travel plans. It's up to you, but I can close my shop now. Seriously, I don't care."

"Wow. I don't know what to say. I'll get back to you right away with my answer."

"Great. And no matter what you choose, the back room is still yours to rent."

"Thanks. I appreciate that you aren't kicking me out."

Charity smiled. "What kind of artist would I be to leave a fellow artist stranded like that? You have gotten way more use out of that space that I ever did. Even for my largest projects. And I would never have rented to you in the first place if I planned to do that. I wanted to give you a trial run before deciding for sure what to do. In my book, you stopping by was perfect timing. I love the things you create. I'm just sorry I don't have room to display anything you make."

"Thank you. I mainly do contract work anyway. And thanks to the new workspace, I can take on even larger projects. I have so enjoyed being here, and I'm glad I won't have to leave."

Charity nodded. "We will talk again when you make up your mind. Now, I need to get back to packing."

Martine looked around the large loft as she ate and reminisced about Charity. Xavier had brought forward some questions that she hadn't thought about for a long time. Where was Charity? And why, after all these years, was she still gone? Finishing her meal, Martine walked down to the shop and looked around. She had a routine that she followed every week. Mondays, the shop was closed all day. That was the day Martine dusted and swept the shop, cleaned up the back room, and then her loft. The rest of the week the shop was only open four hours a day, mostly in the afternoons. Saturday was midday and then closed on Sunday. Following Charity's rules, she could be open or closed as needed. Seldom did the hours change, but occasionally Martine had to be away for her own showings or open-house displays. She wasn't kidding when she told Xavier that business was almost nil. The last two years, especially, had seen very little progress in the way of business in the shop. Martine had kicked around the idea of closing the door completely but just hadn't done so yet. She wasn't sure when the last time was that someone came in to buy something. It wasn't like just anyone off the street could afford Charity's work. The price tags were enough to keep Martine from buying anything herself. She was glad she could enjoy the shop on a daily basis.

Pulling out the sales slip book, Martine noted that it had been six weeks since the last purchase, and two months before that. Both were very small purchases. It was probably past time to close the doors. Charity told her that sales would eventually stop completely. Without her being around to advertise and be out in the public, her works were soon forgotten. She finally made a decision. Martine made a sign to hang in the front window that read, *Open by appointment only*. The store phone was still working. Or she thought it was. She lifted the receiver to make sure it had a dial tone. Smiling, she hung the sign up right above the store phone number that was imprinted on the door. The closed sign would be permanently left in place now.

Glancing at the street in front, the traffic had already died down to just an occasional car or truck. Sighing, Martine felt a bit of relief that there would no longer be any interruptions in her workflow. If Charity wanted the store open more, it was time she returned to do so or hired someone else. Cringing, she felt guilty because that was what the loft was for: in lieu of rental payments, she minded the store. Shaking her head, Martine would have to call or stop at the bank and let someone know to contact Charity about closing the shop and the sign for appointments only. She felt it only right for her to know the change in status.

Sculpting had become a full-time job for Martine over the last couple of years. She had held a part-time job up until the orders became bigger, along with larger paychecks. Now, she could write her own ticket and had a dab of money saved to boot. Heading back to the office, she decided she felt better not to have to worry about the shop anymore. And if Charity returned and wanted to take back the loft—as long as Martine could keep the space to work in—she would be happy. Reaching up to her bun to retrieve the pencil she stuck in there earlier, Martine went back to work.

***

Xavier didn't go too far after leaving Charity's Shoppe. He found an old, dusty truck a block or so down the road to park behind, out of sight, then leaned back in his seat. He had been a little overwhelmed when he walked into the shop. It hadn't changed a bit since the last time he was there, and that was many years ago. He and Charity had been a couple then, and as her fame grew, she spent more and more time going to shows and building her reputation than she did spending time with him. With his ego hurt, they eventually went their separate ways. He used the anger he felt at Charity as an incentive to throw himself into his work. He spent his time expanding his territory in real estate, and now everything had finally come full circle. He was back in the old neighborhood and looking at tearing up the whole blighted area. It was an eyesore, and most of the buildings were empty. Outside of a couple of commercial businesses, there was Charity's Shoppe, smack dab in the middle of things. Surprisingly, that made him pause.

Twenty years earlier, Charity bought her commercial building and the one next door. She wanted to create an artist's paradise. She invited several friends to consider settling into the area, and eventually the art district was born. Old businesses with lofts and big, expansive rooms were perfect for creating masterpieces. Someone bought up a couple of the old buildings to make room for several artists to live and work. Others, like Charity, kept the building all to themselves, creating a beautiful shop to display her vibrant and glimmering pieces. The shop next door was rented to an artist friend who liked living and working in her place of work, just as Charity did. Eventually, the city of Churchtown restored the old downtown and gave incentives to everyone that would move back to the city center. Some did; others closed permanently; the rest stayed. Eventually, traffic was so poor, the starving artists had to quit or move out. That included her friend, who chose to move to a smaller downtown store.

That's when Xavier came in. He began buying the old, dilapidated properties at a premium and planned to tear them all down to build high-end buildings. He hadn't decided yet if the area would suit apartments or a whole new shopping area. His team and the city officials were still hammering that out, but after the city spent all those millions on the downtown project, they weren't going to give in easily to a business center when they could have a new housing project. Either way, there were two old buildings standing in his way, and they both belonged to Charity. As far as he could tell, the extra building was vacant and had been for a long time. Looking through the windows, everything was covered with a layer of dust. He was totally taken aback when he walked into her shop, though. He didn't know why, but Xavier wondered if he thought it would look like she would be closing the shop sometime soon. He had watched the traffic the day before, and no one had stopped by. In fact, one of his team stated that when studying the area, they never saw anyone even drive by the building, yet knew that someone lived there.

Xavier was surprised when the young lady approached him and shook him out of his memories. She wasn't very helpful when he asked for Charity and wondered if she was withholding information. He planned to return the following day and find out for sure, because he needed to get in touch with her about the property. It was quite unfortunate that her buildings sat smack dab in the center of the area. He didn't know how he could work around her buildings, and wondered if Charity would be interested in selling them. Otherwise, Xavier might have to ask if the city would claim imminent domain to get her ousted. It wouldn't be the first time he'd played dirty, but he also didn't want to be in court for years. He had a feeling Charity wouldn't just roll over and sell if she didn't want to. No, indeed. Especially to him. She could be just as intimidating as he was when her back was to the wall. Sighing, he started the car and slowly drove back toward the shop. Stopping to take one more look, he noticed the sign in the window. Jotting down the phone number, he headed back to the hotel to meet up with his team. Needing to put personal feelings aside, Xavier tried to put the problem behind him for the evening. There was plenty of time to worry about Charity and her property.

When Xavier left their relationship, Charity was devastated. Taking into account her lack of personal involvement at the time, she didn't blame him. Fast forward to the subsequent years of business success, she suddenly found herself quite alone. Oh, she still had multiple requests for new projects, and that put plenty of money in the bank. But being alone was the one thing she'd never counted on. After Xavier was gone from her life, she almost didn't notice—what with all the showings to attend and art gallery requests for new lines. Displaying her art was the height of achievement for her, and she basked in the glory. Then the economy went south, and so did her career.

Sitting alone in her breakfast nook, Charity decided she hated being alone and was going to travel or do anything but stay here. Her life had been full of appointments, gallery showings, magazines, and newspaper stories for so long that the silence was stifling. She wasn't sure she knew how to handle it all, and her creativity came to a screeching halt. There hadn't been a new piece added to the gallery in a couple of years, and there were very few sales to put a dent in the overflowing supply. When Martine came to her about renting the back of the shop, she thought that seeing someone else create masterpieces would help her get her mojo back. It didn't. That's when she finally came up with a way to escape. Not that she couldn't just leave anyway, but Martine was as good of an excuse as any. The woman could stay, and Charity could leave it all behind. There were too many memories of Xavier, and too many thoughts of her career coming to a complete stop. Too much of everything. And thankfully, she left it all to a willing Martine to deal with.

***

The following morning, Xavier attended meetings with several different businessmen. When money came to town, they all wanted a piece of the pie. He looked around as his staff asked all the appropriate questions and managed to frustrate most of the men. Xavier wasn't going to blindly throw money at projects at their say-so, and he knew going in that no one was going to go away happy. He knew most of these men because they had attended many of Charity's events in the past. He assumed several even owned some of her creations. He wasn't sure whether any of them remembered him or not. Normally, he stood off in a corner and was only seen when Charity wanted him around. The gossip pages referred to him as her escort and alluded to other things, but nothing was ever caught on photos to back it up. Not for a lack of trying on their part. By the time Charity became well known, Xavier was an afterthought in her life.

Thankfully, by the time lunch was served, he only had one more meeting and that was with the mayor. He certainly wasn't going to ruffle his feathers at this stage of the game. Xavier was almost done eating by the time the mayor arrived and ordered his own lunch.

"I'm sorry, Xavier. I had an emergency to handle as I walked out the door. Then the noon traffic was ridiculous. Maybe you should get into the highway business and build a loop around town."

Xavier wiped his mouth and took a drink to wash down his last bite. "I'm pretty sure that is way out of my scope of work. You'll have to talk to someone else about the traffic problems."

The mayor sighed. "I know. There is always something that needs done, and sadly it takes forever." Smiling, he thanked the waitress for his drink. "Down to business. I have heard both sides of the argument for building a new business district or putting up housing, and you know the way I am leaning. Besides, that area is blighted, and I can give you special tax incentives for housing. Access to the main highway is right there, and it would be easy for everyone to get to work."

"Or cause more traffic congestion in the area."

"There is that," Mayor Spears chuckled. "That's all we need. More traffic problems. Anyway, I'm sure your men have mentioned that housing will be an easy way to get your project off the ground."

"Yes. We also sat here this morning listening to men drooling over the possibility of getting me to support their pet projects, so I dismissed my staff to go have a leisurely meal so they didn't have to listen to one more business meeting. I appreciate you being straightforward with me as to which way the wind blows. It really makes no difference to me which direction I go at this point. But I do have two properties I have been unable to obtain so I can clear the area."

"Oh, yes. Ms. Charity Hannibal's properties. You know her, don't you?"

"It's been many years since I have seen or heard from her. Do you have any idea how to get in touch with her?"

"I have no idea. Last time I saw her was at a gallery

event, and I believe my wife spent a fortune on something of hers."

"Yes, she does beautiful art, for sure. I guess I'll have to go back to her shop to see what I can find out. So far I've come up empty."

"You mean it's still open? I heard she left town."

"I stopped yesterday afternoon to look over the buildings, and someone was running the store for her. The gal, uh, Martine, I guess it is, said she had no idea where Charity was. I find that hard to believe, so I need to go and visit again."

"Well, good luck. Just know that the city is ready whenever you are to get the ball rolling out there. It's quite a mess and we'd sure like to get it cleaned up. Especially at someone else's expense. It won't take us long to get rezoning since we are all on the same page."

"That's good to hear. I'll leave you to the rest of your meal. I need to get busy and find Charity."

The men shook hands and Xavier stopped by the booth where his staff was sitting. Chatting for a moment, he then left the men to begin the process of drawing up plans for apartments, condos, townhouses, or whatever was best that would fit the area. Maybe a mixture, even. After all, he owned four full blocks, except for the two parcels that Charity owned. He planned to take care of that problem himself. He had refrained from asking Mayor Spears about eminent domain. Xavier would save that for the nuclear option, if and when he got to that point.

The drive back out to his properties was irritating. The mayor was right: traffic was terrible. He'd have to find a different route to go back to the hotel. Pulling off and taking the access road, Xavier sat in a big parking lot and looked around. Most of the buildings were showing wear and tear. He wasn't sure, but many of them looked at if they had been broken into. Windows were shattered in the old factories, and he could see pigeons roosting around the openings. He was sure the buildings would be a nightmare to walk into and pitied his workmen. Driving slowly around the property, he noted a couple of buildings that must have been recently evacuated, since they were in much better shape. Getting out, he walked to one and looked through the dirty window. The open front was large, and looked as if it was still a solid structure. He wondered what the place looked like inside as thoughts began to formulate. By the time he had driven around and investigated several buildings from the outside, his brain was working overtime. Picking up the phone, he called Rainy, his office manager.

"I need to get a hold of the keys to the buildings in Churchtown. What can you tell me?"

"Let's see. The realtor we went through for purchasing was going to mail them to our office. Let me see if we have them yet. I believe he was going to hang on to them until we signed on the dotted line for the last of the buildings."

Xavier heard the phone being placed on hold and waited, while standing outside of Charity's extra building. It too, looked in decent shape, although both of the buildings could use a new paint job. He hoped the inside was in as good as shape as her shop next door. He remembered Charity had hired a reputable designer and the best carpenters she could find to remodel her loft. He wondered if the empty building had been similarly remodeled at the same time. Funny. He guessed he had never seen the inside of this building before. He shrugged his shoulders as Rainy came back to the phone.

"Boss, we don't have them. I gave the realtor a quick call and he has them ready to mail, but I told him you were in the area and would have someone stop and get them. I took the liberty to call Buck to take care of that detail and deliver them to you."

"Perfect. I can always count on you to get things done. While I wait, I'll try to find the woman who owns the last two buildings. Unless you want to work on that for me?"

Rainy laughed. "Sure. Give me her name, social, and bank account number."

Xavier smiled. "Right. I'll get back with you." He chuckled. "Actually, I may not need to find her. I may be veering off our path."

"That wouldn't be the first time."

"True. Thanks again, Rainy. You're the best."

"I know, and I keep waiting for that big raise that never comes. I have a kid almost ready for college, you know."

"I know, you ungrateful woman. What about that bonus I gave you at Christmas?"

"That puny thing? That hardly put the holiday food on the table for my family."

Xavier gave a hearty belly laugh. Rainy never ceased to tease him unmercifully. She was the only one that could get away with it too. "Okay, okay. Maybe the Easter Bunny will bring you a goodie basket."

"Boy, I hope so."

"Bye, Rainy. Thanks again."

Tucking his phone in his pocket, Xavier walked next door and noted the closed sign, along with a new sign about opening for appointments only. He knocked on the door and waited. Then he pounded on the door and waited some more. He repeated his actions several times, with no response. Then he called the shop's phone number, but it always wound up going to voicemail. He didn't leave a message, but called back several times, pounding on the door in between. Becoming quite frustrated, he was literally mad as a hornet by the time he saw Martine coming to the door. He put his phone away and waited impatiently as she headed toward him.

Jerking the door open, Martine wasn't any happier than Xavier. She practically screamed at him, "What do you want?"

Surprised at her anger, he matched it. "I need to talk to you."

"What? You can't read?" She pointed to the sign in the window of the door.

"I can read, but I need to talk to you right now."

"Make an appointment." She slammed the door in his

face, and had it locked before he could respond.

As Martine stomped away, he yelled, "Hey! I need to talk to you! Come back here!"

Martine threw up her hands and stormed into the back room. She was livid, but so was Xavier. He called the phone number several times and finally gave up, leaving his phone number on his last try. Fuming, he walked to his car and paced while waiting for Buck to show up. He was still in a foul mood when Buck arrived with the keys. Buck knew better than to ask what had happened. Instead, they dug through the box and began checking out a few of the nicer buildings. After they looked at two, Buck called in the rest of the team, and everyone began doing a thorough review of what they had. The commercial buildings that were used by the birds were left alone. No one wanted to get close to them, and they would be torn down no matter what. But ideas were forming, and the team was all on board to revamp their ideas for the area once again.

Xavier stood at his car and looked around while the men were talking and scheming. The four of them had been with him for a long time, and the best thing was, they weren't yes-men. If they didn't agree or like an idea Xavier had, they told him so. Their relationships were only stronger because of it too. Technically, between these four and Rainy, they were the only people he could trust. The more money he made, the closer his circle of friends became. He had to learn that the hard way, but it benefited all of them in the end. Buck was like a brother to him, and the other three men were contracted to design all of Xavier's projects. A past designer had leaked information to a competitor and their competing bid was offered to undercut Xavier's, costing his company a great amount of money when they lost the job. He cut ties with the designer's firm immediately.

***

Martine was livid. How dare the man pound on the door and think he was more special than anyone else. He could make an appointment if he wanted to talk. He wasn't there to buy anything, anyway. She wasn't sure what he wanted with Charity, but she was glad she had no idea how to get a hold of the woman. Standing there, staring at her latest project, it ticked her off that she was interrupted. Yes, it was the template for her newest statue, but it was just as important as if she was working on the real thing. Now she was too mad to get back to work. She let out a loud growl and ran up the steps two at a time to the loft. Martine pulled a pitcher of lemonade out of the refrigerator and poured herself a large glass. She slowly sipped and calmed herself down. A few snacks and another glass of lemonade later, she figured she might be good company now.

Picking up her purse, it was time to head over to the bank to locate the individual that took care of Charity's account. Martine had forgotten her name as she hadn't talked to her in a year or more. As she began to pull away from the shop, she realized that Xavier and several others were looking at the buildings surrounding her. Pausing, she wondered what all that was about. On the drive to the bank, she began to put two and two together. The man had probably bought a couple of buildings and wanted to buy Charity's. What else could it be? She figured she'd better mention that to the banker too. Something was going on, for sure.

2

Charity watched from an upstairs window and could see Xavier walking around with his minions. Something was happening, and she wasn't happy not knowing the answers. There was too much activity going on around the shop and not enough information coming forward to her. She puzzled on it for quite a while before giving up. Hoping Martine would come through with the information first, she sat back and waited.

The empty building had been calling her name for a long time. She was tired of being on the road, roaming from place to place. Available only by phone, she began to wonder if running away had worked at all. She hadn't received any calls for a long time. A few minor repairs, a message about a large deposit or two into her account by Martine, and little else. Her cell phone was something she picked up off the shelf and renewed her minutes as she needed them. That was the only number she gave out these days, and it was only for emergencies or reservations. If someone recognized her, she moved on. After the first couple of years, Charity realized that no amount of running was going to help her be happy again. And her creative juices still weren't flowing. That's when she finally began to get treatment for her depression. It was only then that she remained in one location longer than a few months. Now here she was, looking out her own window, but still in hiding. She shook her head and walked back to the living room to mope.

She didn't want to intrude on Martine's life. A few months earlier, she hired someone to clean the empty building next to the shop so she would have a place to stay while in town. One day she hoped to be brave enough to return permanently. Charity monitored Martine's career from afar and was happy to see her building a thriving business. Maybe it was time to ask her move into the spare building and open her own shop. So far, it looked as if Martine managed to stay out of the limelight, except for when presenting her masterpieces. Charity hoped the girl wouldn't get tarnished by all the glitter and fawning that happens when fame hits.

She walked to the window to peek out once again. It looked like everyone was gone now. Finally. When it was close to dark, her plan was to leave once again for a few months. Although she hadn't figured out where. Tired of meandering, she wondered if she was ready to face the community and the world once again. Maybe she wouldn't have to. Hopefully, most people had forgotten about her by now. Then her phone rang and startled her out of her dreaming. Looking down, she noted the bank's number.

"This is Charity."

"Yes, this is Georgia at First National. I wanted to let you know about something that happened today at the shop. I have Martine in my office and, if it's okay with you, I'd like to have her explain it and then if you have questions you can ask her directly."

Charity paused only for a second. There was no better

time than the present. "Yes. That's fine. Put her on." She could hear the phone being passed in the background.

"Charity? It's Martine. How are you?"

"I'm just fine. How are things going for you? I see you are making a name for yourself."

Martine blushed. "Thank you. I'm doing well. And I couldn't do it without the space you rented to me. It has been a godsend all these years."

"Wonderful. So, tell me what's going on?"

"Yesterday, a man walked into the store and asked for you. Of course, I couldn't tell him anything because I don't know anything. He gave his name as Xavier and said he knew you. I didn't think much about it, but after our short visit, I got to wondering about the shop itself. It has been six weeks since I sold anything, and all the stores have either closed or moved out of the area. I don't get any foot traffic these days, and that's when I decided to put up a sign that said appointments only and hung it up above the phone number. I hope that is all right."

"That's fine, Martine. I'm surprised you waited this long."

She breathed a sigh of relief. "I'm glad. I get a lot more work done when I'm not interrupted. Which brings me to today. I was in the back working and could hear knocking on the door. I ignored it, even though it was getting louder all the time. Then the phone kept ringing. I couldn't work with all the racket, so I headed to the door. It was the same guy from yesterday. He was mad that I wouldn't answer the door or the phone, and I was mad that he interrupted my work. Anyway, I wasn't very nice to him. Yelling, I told him to leave a message. Then I slammed the door in his face and stomped off, leaving him there to scream at me through the door. I'm sorry. I probably shouldn't have done that, but I knew he wasn't a customer. All he wanted was to find out where you were, anyway." She blew out her breath and then sighed.

Charity could see why Martine was mad—plus, Xavier never did like being ignored. She chuckled. "Sounds like you were both upset, but it's not like you could tell him anything. What did he do after that?"

"Let's see. I took some time to cool off. I couldn't work after all that, so I paced and did a few things in the loft. I eventually decided I'd better go to the bank and talk to Georgia. When I began to pull out, he was with a bunch of other guys looking at the empty properties on the block. I don't know if they are buying them or what, because I didn't see a realtor. But they had keys to get inside. On my way over to the bank, I wondered if they'd bought some of the property around here and that was why Xavier wanted to talk to you. I asked Georgia if she could find out."

"Thanks for the update. Don't bother talking to him again. By the way, I do know him. He is in real estate, so he probably is buying up the area. I'll talk to Georgia about what's happening. And by the way, do you still have your same phone number?"

"Yeah."

"Great. I need to take care of a few things, but I'll get

back to you soon. Okay?"

"That's fine. It was good to visit with you, even under these circumstances. I miss some of our long conversations. I took your words of wisdom to heart and am trying to stay grounded."

"Impressive. I will talk to you soon. Now hand the phone back to Georgia."

Charity heard a little bit of the conversation between the two before catching the click of the door shutting behind her as she left. Georgia was on the line once again.

"What do you want me to do, Charity?"

"Are you busy right now?"

"No, I don't have any appointments on my calendar right now. Why?"

"I'm going to stop by."

"You're in town?"

Charity laughed. "Yeah. I'll be there in a bit."

"Looking forward to it."

Instead of waiting for darkness as planned, Charity left before Martine got back home. She took a circuitous route to the bank and went inside. Wearing a big floppy hat and sunglasses, even the front-office girls didn't know who she was. Georgia was waiting for her to walk in the door and led her back without Charity needing to give her name. Once behind closed doors, the two hugged. They had been friends forever, so who else was Charity going to turn to?

"It's so good to see you again. We need to get together

so you can tell me all the wonderful stories of where you traveled since I saw you last."

"We will. I'm not sure how long I'll be here this trip. In fact, I was getting ready to leave town when you called. Now I'm not sure what I should do. I'm torn, actually."

"The way Martine made it sound, you might need to stick around. Sounds like Xavier is throwing his money into the real estate market here. I heard someone was buying up property, but I didn't put two and two together until she walked in the door with her news."

"There are some buildings that deserve to be torn down in my neighborhood, but not all of them. What's the latest gossip?"

"According to the papers, someone has been buying all the property for four blocks around you. They have been discussing with Mayor Spears what they will be allowed to do. The only mention of your property was to say that you still held the titles. I hadn't read the articles very closely until today, while I was waiting for you to arrive."

"So that's why he wanted to find me. To buy my buildings."

"Probably. I have no idea, though. Are you going to talk to him?"

Charity leaned back in her chair and stared at the ceiling for a few moments. "I don't know. I haven't seen Xavier for ten years, give or take." Sitting back up and facing Georgia, she said, "I'm not sure what to do. He was angry when he left, and I didn't even notice. What kind of a girlfriend was I to not even care that he was gone, and I how was pushing him out of my life?"

Georgia shook her head. "We all make mistakes, my dear."

"But this was a huge one. One that ruined our relationship, all because I had stars in my eyes. Parties, accolades, money flowing into my account, TV, and newspaper accounts of all my accomplishments. I mean, I got sucked up into the limelight and even the threat of losing Xavier didn't bring me down until much later. Too much later." She looked at Georgia. "You tried to warn me, and I didn't listen."

"I know. And then you tried to run away and hide. How's that working out for you?"

"Harsh, Georgia." She shook her head. "Although I deserve every bit of it."

"I'm sorry."

"No. I'm sorry. You were right. It didn't work out for me. And I haven't learned a thing, evidently, since I planned on leaving tonight after I saw Xavier poking around the neighborhood this afternoon."

"Now we are getting to the bottom of the problem: Xavier. You need to face him and apologize, you know."

"Says you and my therapist."

"Smart therapist." Georgia chuckled. "Stay. Talk to Martine and catch up with her. Look over your old shop and decide what you really want to do. And I have a feeling Xavier is going to be around off and on if he really has bought all that property. It's time to stop running and talk to him. You don't have to sell out to him, but you do need to tell him how you feel."

"I'm sure it's too late for us, but you're right. I need to talk to him. I'm pretty sure it might be one ugly conversation."

"It doesn't matter how ugly. Apologize for being laser-focused on your career and losing sight of what was really important. He can either accept the apology or not. But as long as you're sincere, you will have done your part and be able to move on with your life."

"Move on with my life. Interesting concept. I thought that was what I was doing when I left town."

Georgia got up, came around her desk, and perched on a corner. "How about you come over to the house tonight for drinks and supper? I'll call and tell Maurice to fix another plate."

"You still have Maurice? Wow. I love his cooking. I don't know how you can afford him, but I'm not turning that invitation down."

"Maurice loves us. Besides, my husband will never let him go. He hates my cooking, and he can't boil water. So what choice do we have?"

Charity laughed. An honest-to-goodness laugh. Unlike the last several years, it was a laughter of joy and love toward her old friend. It felt good, too. "I'll be there by seven."

"Right on time. Now get out of here so I can finish up and be home before you arrive."

They hugged and gave each other a rub on the back. Charity walked out feeling one hundred percent better than when she had walked in. It was good to be with a true friend again, and it was way overdue. She went back to her temporary quarters and pulled into the garage. It was nice to be able to hide away. The loft apartment was set up differently than the one above her shop. This one had solar lights on the stairwell, charged by the skylights on the roof. She didn't even need to turn on a light until she got into the apartment. The windows already had blackout curtains, left by the former tenants. Shutting the door, she flipped the switch and a soft light illuminated the space. Throwing her purse and keys on the coffee table, she decided to go take a shower and change for supper. Dinner at Georgia's wasn't formal, but she did want to look nice. She hadn't seen Gary in years. On her drive across the country and back, she would stop by the bank occasionally to see Georgia. Plus, they talked on the phone at least once a month. Georgia was the only person she would answer the phone for, unless she was expecting a call from her travel agent.

Now that her bank account was beginning to drain from all her travels, Charity needed to make a decision. She needed to stay in one place for one thing. She also needed to sell the multitude of inventory in the shop. Or at least a good portion of it. Did she want to sell her buildings to Xavier? Where would she live if she sold? Of course, the money she received for the buildings would set her up nicely elsewhere. What a conundrum.

She'd discuss it with Georgia and Gary this evening. Gary was in high finance and would be able to help her decide what to do. He helped her set up her stock portfolio, and there was no way she would touch that. She needed to earn more money. And soon. With her creative juices still in hiding, there were tough decisions to make. Sighing, she headed for the shower.

When Maurice found out Charity would be having supper with his employers, he went all out to fix a special meal. He whipped up a cheesecake for dessert and hoped his rushing around wouldn't ruin it. Maurice was as fond of Charity as he was Georgia and Gary. She appreciated his meals and didn't hesitate to tell him so. Besides, she treated him well, unlike so many other people who had been invited in the past, many of whom were no longer invited back due to their rude behavior toward him. After catching up over the meal and visiting at length with Maurice, the three went to the study for coffee and dessert. The cheesecake came out as luscious as ever. Even though she was stuffed, Charity asked for seconds, which put Maurice over the moon. Not to be outdone, Gary asked for thirds, but Maurice slapped his hand and told him no. Everyone laughed as Maurice stuck his nose in the air and stalked out of the room with the dirty plates. He was soon back with a carryout container holding the rest of the cheesecake for Charity. That set off a round of complaints from Gary, but Maurice paid him no mind.

Gary quit pouting and settled into his chair before

saying what was on everyone's mind. "Okay, Charity. Spit it out. What do you need help with?"

"Good question, Gary. Thanks for getting right to the point."

Smirking, he replied, "No problem."

"I came back to check on a few things. I waited for Martine to leave and went over to check the store. She keeps it clean, but there is still a lot of merchandise sitting around. Without advertising, I suppose people have pretty much given up on me. I need to do one of two things: reopen and advertise to get rid of everything, or reopen and begin to take special orders again. I don't think I want to stock the store anymore. It has more inventory than it should, and I may never get rid of it all."

Georgia interrupted. "You only offered two options. What about Xavier wanting to buy your property?"

Gary glanced between the two women. "Whoa. I must have missed something here. Xavier?"

"He's been sniffing around the area, and we believe he may have bought some properties. You know what that means. Tear down and redevelop."

"You haven't talked to him, then?"

"No. Have you?"

"Nope. How do you know he bought property by your shop?"

"Martine had the pleasure of his acquaintance and he demanded to talk to me. Then I saw him and his crew looking at other properties in the area today, so I suppose he wants to buy mine so he can level the whole area and start from fresh. You know how he goes in and buys blighted areas and redoes everything. There is nothing wrong with that, except it's my property we are talking about. And I'm not even sure he has purchased the others—except they didn't have a realtor with them and were able to go in and out of the buildings. I was busy cleaning the apartment and repacking, so I didn't notice them until later in the day. When Georgia and Martine called from the bank, I was able to leave sight unseen because Xavier and his crew were gone by then."

"Well, buying large parcels does sound like Xavier's modus operandi."

Georgia cleared her throat. "I, uh, called Mayor Spears after you left the bank."

"You did?"

"Yes. Well, I know you wanted me to find out, so I went right to the source instead of snooping around. I explained that, as a banker, I thought I should know if people were going to want loans on property around that area, and I needed to know if it was going to be commercial or residential."

"And?" Both Gary and Charity leaned toward her in anticipation.

"It is Xavier, and the paper is right. He has already purchased four blocks, and your two properties are the only thing standing in his way from demolishing the whole works."

Charity screeched, "And you couldn't have mentioned this when we first started to discuss it?"

"I hated to tell you. The thing is, you don't have to sell. After all, it is your property."

Gary butted in. "Unless the esteemed mayor deems it necessary to use eminent domain."

Charity and Georgia both gasped. "He wouldn't dare," Georgia spat out. "We can make his life miserable if he tries."

Gary nodded. "True, but it's been done before."

Charity shook her head. "This changes everything. Or nothing. I'm going to have to talk to Xavier, aren't I?"

Georgia reached over and patted her hand. "I'm afraid so. And soon. We need to approach this whole thing logically. You have a store, a career on hold, and a renter who adores the space she is in, with a busy artistic life of her own. This decision affects a lot more than just you."

"Yes, it does." She let out a big yawn. "I'd better go back to the apartment. I have some serious thinking to do, but I'm too tired to do it tonight."

They all got up and walked to Charity's car. "Try to get some rest. Keep us informed, and we are here to help you with whatever you need."

"Thanks. I know that." Lifting her carryout box, she said, "Tell Maurice thank you for me." Gary tried to grab it out of her hands when she reached over to give them hugs. "You wouldn't dare tick off Maurice, now, would you?"

Gary sighed, and Charity jumped into her car while she had the chance. She grinned and held up her precious box as she sped off, laughing at Gary's frown. Gary and

Georgia walked back inside, and all they could do was hope Charity talked to Xavier sooner rather than later.

Tossing and turning while trying to get comfortable for most of the night, Charity attempted to come to a decision about Xavier. When she walked into the bathroom that morning, she squinted against the harsh lighting as she warmed up the water for her washcloth. Scrubbing her face, she finally got a good look in the mirror. What reflected back to her looked like a racoon. Peering closer, she was disgusted. Yes, a racoon. Charity had forgotten to remove her makeup before she went to bed and proceeded to smear mascara all over her eyes and down her cheeks. One look at the washcloth told her everything she needed to know. She let out a growl of disgust, then began to scrub not only the washcloth but her face. Fifteen minutes later, her face was rosy and clean, but the washcloth was thrown in the trash. There was no way all that black was going to come out.

Now that she was wide awake, it was time to fortify herself with some breakfast and a large cup of coffee or two. She pushed back the blinds to look out the window. It was going to be a respectable day, and there was no reason to stay holed up inside. She needed to handle her life right here and now. Charity decided to make a plan to move home. She smiled. *Home. I like the sound of that. I do have a home. Why am I running around when I have a perfectly nice home here? Two homes, at that.*

For some reason, even though the day started off so badly, somewhere along the way she made a decision.

Once dressed, she grabbed her keys and headed next door to the shop. It was time to set foot in the place without sneaking around and work out the problems. The bell tinkled as she walked through the door, and it put another smile on her face. She hadn't realized how much she missed that sound. Slowly walking through the shop, she realized she was no longer alone.

"Charity? Is that really you?"

"Sure is, Martine." They met in the middle of the space and hugged.

After pulling away, Martine exclaimed, "I hope you aren't kicking me out."

"Heavens, no. I'm actually staying at my place next door. But I needed to see the shop this morning to make some decisions."

"You're staying next door? I saw some activity over there a few months ago and thought I had a new neighbor. Then I didn't see anybody around after a few days."

"I paid someone to do some cleaning and repairs on the place so I could stay there when I came to town. They did a nice job, although I did have to throw away a washcloth this morning." Martine looked at her oddly, and Charity waved it off. "Never mind. Anyway, it's past time to make a decision about all my merchandise sitting here getting dusty. But it looks like you have taken good care of the place."

"That was my Monday project. Clean and sweep. It's easier when you don't have anyone coming in to leave fingerprints everywhere."

Chuckling, Charity agreed. "Over time, I had forgotten the huge number of items still here. I'll need to talk to someone about a show or do something to get rid of this stuff. Good heavens. What was I thinking? I evidently wasn't in a minimalist era."

Martine couldn't help but laugh. "Come on back to the studio. I'm in the middle of a new project I want you to see."

"Great. I love your sculptures. Who is this one for?"

"Mr. Parker is the one who solicited it, but it is for the park downtown." They stepped into the back room, and Martine stood back while Charity walked around the partially finished statue. Representing the park, the sculpted tree would have birds, a squirrel or two, and some flowers at the base. Martine wasn't sure if she would be able to add anything else but hoped to hide a little something in the leaves.

"This is the best work you have ever done, Martine. I mean it. This is fabulous, and I'll be thrilled to see it in the park."

Martine grinned. "You think so?"

"I saw your earlier works. And I've seen pictures of some of your newer ones, but this one, my dear, will definitely make a name for you. Not like people don't know about you anyway. Mr. Parker would never have commissioned your work if he hadn't approved of other work he had seen."

"Thank you for the compliment. It has helped to not worry about the shop while I'm back here working. I have gotten a lot more done, now that I don't have to worry about someone interrupting. Not like there was much business, but I always worried the bell wouldn't work and someone would walk out the door with something when I wasn't looking. That's why I never worked back here while I was minding the shop."

"Have no fear. That is no longer a problem for you. You can forget about the phone and store both. You have bigger things to take care of. By the way, has the loft been comfortable?"

"It's great. I haven't changed a thing. I brought my own things over, of course, but it's been perfect. Especially while I'm working. I lose track of time and sometimes I'm down here until the wee hours. I'm glad I don't have to drive home afterward."

"Good. You can stay. I like the loft next door too. I think I'll just remain there."

"Are you going to be back permanently?"

"I haven't decided on that yet. There is one more big thing I need to figure out first."

"What's that?"

"Xavier."

"Oh, yes. I forgot about him."

"Did he leave you a card?"

"No. But his phone number is on the answering machine from when I wouldn't talk to him the other day."

She nodded. "I'll get it from there. Now, don't let me disturb you. I might be in and out of here, so you might want to keep the door shut between you and the workshop, so you aren't disturbed."

"I'll do that. And that way you will know I'm in there too. Otherwise, I'll leave it open."

"Great. Now. I need to make a few calls and see what I can do about my precious inventory."

The two went their separate ways to work. Charity took down Xavier's phone number and chuckled at how exasperated he sounded with Martine. Then, she called her favorite gallery owner to set up an appointment. He was more than happy to stop over to see her displays and work out a new showing. In fact, he was almost giddy. Charity laughed at him and arranged to meet him at the store at two that afternoon. After a few more strolls around the shop, Charity went outside and stood on the sidewalk looking at both of her properties. They were looking drab and unkempt. It was no wonder Xavier was thinking of tearing it all down. She shook her head and decided to take matters into her own hands.

Going back to her loft, she sat down and made a few calls. With appointments set up for the next couple of days, she decided to make one more call. The landlord at her current apartment was disappointed to hear Charity was moving out, and he was willing to make sure someone packed up her belongings and have them shipped to her. They chose to order a moving container, and he would hire some young men to get the unit loaded. She was more than happy to have it all done for her. For a fee, of course. Once the container arrived, she could hire someone to move her belongings into the loft.

Despite not getting any more sleep than she did, Charity felt that the best decisions were made between her tossing and turning. Not once had she regretted following through. She figured that was a good sign. The only thing she put off was contacting Xavier. She knew it was only a matter of time before he showed up on her doorstep, anyway.

By two, she was back at the gallery showing Mr. Piedmont around. "As you can see, I am way overstocked. I have sold very little the last few years, but that's my own fault for dropping off the radar."

"Yes, and you didn't leave me a thing to sell, either. I was so disappointed because I wanted to set up a new showing."

"Well, you can do it now."

"To be honest, sweetheart, we have enough here for more than one showing."

Sheepishly, Charity agreed. "I know. I think I was using this as more of a storage unit by the way it looks. The presentation isn't very appealing."

"I'll fix that. I will send the staff over to haul several different sizes back to the gallery. I'll return and tag the ones I want so they will know what to start with."

"When do you think you'll set a date?"

"As soon as possible. I have a current showing, and the person I was working with for right after this one is being hard to get along with. I'm so done with him. He can go to my competitor and drive him crazy. I'd say in about six weeks we can have a full-blown gala."

"That soon?"

"Honey, I know a good thing when I see it. And I'm dying to be the one to bring you back into the limelight again."

"Now don't get too carried away. I haven't created anything in several years, and I have no desire to do so right now. No commissions, understand?"

"Got it. We have more than enough for people to choose from. Now, let me meander a bit to get a feel of the items and what I want to choose."

Charity left Mr. Piedmont wandering around the store while she looked over her ledger. Martine kept meticulous notes about any sales, and she was pleased to see everything in order. A half hour later, Mr. Piedmont gave Charity a kiss on both cheeks and said he would call the shop and leave a message when he'd set a definite date for the showing. Charity begged off giving out a personal number right now. That was something she needed to tend to in the next couple of weeks. Maybe when her belongings arrived, she would feel more like getting a permanent number. In the meantime, she would keep her secret phone. After all, she did have the shop phone where people could call and leave messages. Once word got out that she was back in town, she was afraid the phone would ring off the hook and disturb Martine. Walking over to the phone, she muted the bell. Now, it could ring to its hearts content and people could leave messages. She'd have to check on it occasionally. At least it had a flashing light, so you knew if there were messages or not.

She was just heading out the door when Martine walked through. "Hey. I'm glad I caught you. I'm going to be in and out of here every day, and the gallery is going to come get some things one of these days. I'm sorry if the hubbub disturbs you."

"No problem. Maybe a little noise will be good for me. The silence is sometimes spooky. Especially when an odd noise happens."

"I understand completely. Oh. I almost forgot. I turned the shop ringer off, and we will let everyone leave a voicemail. I got to thinking that once people know I'm back, they will call this number since I gave up my other one."

"Nice. I appreciate that. It always made me jump when it rang. Usually, it was a telemarketer or spam call anyway. And by the way, since I'm not manning the shop, we need to renegotiate my lease to include the loft."

Charity waved her hands around. "Pish posh. Until I get everything sold out of my shop, we don't need to discuss it. I have to run the utilities anyway. We can discuss it later."

"You sure? I'm fine with increasing my rent now."

"I'm good. We can work on that in a few months. You concentrate on that sculpture and let me worry about the rest of the place. Including whatever Xavier has up his sleeve."

"Good. I don't need to walk into that hornet's nest again." Martine looked greatly relieved.

"You let me deal with him. I've known him for years and can be just as stubborn. Now then, I'll let you get back to whatever you were going to do. I'll lock up behind me."

An increase in rent would be a good thing right now, but having the shop and people running around was not conducive to a renter dealing with it. No, she would wait until things settled down. Besides, Charity didn't know what Xavier was going to do to cause problems for her in the near future. Not yet anyway.

3

The next two weeks remained busy for Charity as she dealt with getting construction bids and repricing the items in the showroom. On the advice of Mr. Piedmont, she raised the prices on some of her exquisite items and lowered them on others, which might entice people to pick up a few at bargain rates. Once customers were seen buying the lower-priced items, it encouraged others to buy a higher priced piece, so they weren't outdone by their acquaintances. Jealousy tended to make Charity a few extra bucks at those showings. Looking back, she realized how ridiculous the whole thing was, but it put money in her bank account, and she guessed that was all that mattered in the end. Of course, the gallery received a huge cut too.

Xavier hadn't shown up yet, which Charity was grateful for. She wanted to be in the middle of, or at the end of, her current remodeling projects before he came by. Still, not knowing his end game, she was more than willing to make it as difficult as possible for him to obtain her property. She wondered why she was being so spiteful when their breakup was mostly her fault. But she didn't want to think of that, so anytime she began to wallow in self-pity, she got busy going through her artwork. Occasionally a glimmer of creativity would hit as she polished and placed new prices on her items. But it would soon leave when she thought of stepping into her workshop. The drive to continue inventing new pieces seemed to be just out of reach.

She created additions and changes to her brand new spreadsheet as she listed each piece one by one. Charity had always done her own bookwork. She had no desire to hire someone to keep track of her money. People were way too nosy for their own good. At least she knew her CPA was honest and never said a word about her being a client.

By the end of the month, a crew was siding both properties and putting on new roofs and gutters. She picked a high-end product for everything, knowing it would pay off in the end. No more painting required was a plus. Choosing pleasant colors, the two properties would blend yet be noticeably separate from each other. Similar in construction, it always made sense to Charity to own them both. The heating and cooling units were replaced when she first bought the buildings, so those were still functioning well. Somewhere along the line she had the plumbing replaced too. The lofts didn't need much work, but after all these years, she wondered about replacing carpet. In the meantime, she needed to prepare for her show at the gallery.

When the moving container showed up with her belongings, Charity sweet-talked some of the construction crew to move her things inside on the main floor and the heaviest items up the stairs to the loft. As she dug through her clothes, she picked out many outfits and threw them back in boxes to be donated. With a clear head now, Charity wasn't sure why she had been dragging around all these boxes that she hadn't opened in years. Calling Georgia, they set a date to go shopping for a new outfit for the gallery showing, which was coming up in a couple of weeks.

It seemed so sudden when things became quiet around the area. But crew after crew were completing their jobs and packing up to leave. Charity stood on the sidewalk and looked at her properties. One was seafoam green. The color was so soft that it magically changed colors as the sun moved into different positions. The other was so pale a yellow you weren't sure if it was yellow or white. The trim on both were complementary colors. The front windows were replaced with double paned tinted glass to keep out the heat and cold. Charity was anxious to find large drapes to match the color of the buildings. That was going to be difficult, and wondered if she would have to have them custom made. She also had the siding crew take down the Charity's Shoppe sign and put it in the back room. Although drab and beat up by the weather, she didn't want to replace it nor throw it away. Her days of having a showroom were done, but she certainly wanted the keepsake. The front doors were original to the buildings, and they were very ornate. But she'd had special one-way tinted glass installed as replacements. She could have left the old glass, but they were showing signs of small cracks inching their way in several spots. One big bang, and that would be the end of them. It was probably a good thing the empty building hadn't been used for a long time and that she was using a back entrance, because the front-door glass was in exceptionally bad shape.

Now that Mr. Piedmont had taken a third of her inventory to the gallery, Charity realized how drab the walls were. She decided to paint them herself but would wait to start until after the showing. After all, she had no idea how many items would be returned to the shop. Deciding to keep to the seafoam color on the outside, she thought the light color would be quite attractive on the walls. The scuffed-up floor was beyond help, and until everything was safely out of the room, she couldn't replace it anyway. Little by little, she was moving the smaller items into groupings. The larger ones would need two people to move, and she didn't want to bother Martine since she was working so hard to finish her own project. The showcases would be the most difficult to move, but Martine agreed to help her when she was ready.

The shopping trip was successful. Her new slinky black dress fit without showing all the extra pounds she had put on over the last few years. It came with a wrap that could be thrown off or left on as needed. It was so light and airy, Charity decided that it was a beautiful accent to leave on, and Georgia agreed. Her friend found a raspberry dress similar in style and decided they should celebrate their success by going out for drinks.

Before she knew it, the day of her showing arrived. Mr. Piedmont sent a limo around to pick up Charity. She had convinced Martine to come with her and do a little shmoozing while there. Martine didn't have to be asked twice. She also went shopping and found a pale gold outfit that went well with her hair coloring. She waited at Charity's for the limo and was almost as nervous as she was. She thought it great fun to arrive in the limo and knew people would be wondering who she was and why she arrived with Charity, so they made up stories as to who she was on their ride to the gallery. The chauffeur snorted at a couple of the outlandish tales they came up with, which made the women giggle all the harder; the laughter helped alleviate both their nerves for the ride over.

Soon, they arrived and were led inside by Mr. Piedmont. There were many people taking pictures of the two women as they got out of the limo and walked inside. Charity prepared Martine ahead of time that the media would be at the event. After all, Charity had been gone a long time. As Mr. Piedmont led her to her spot in the gallery, Martine wandered off by herself to look around. She heard whispers, wondering who she was. She smiled and knew that, eventually, someone would get up the nerve to ask. As she walked around a pillar, she ran into Xavier, peeking around the other side at Charity. She smirked and waited a moment while thinking about what to say to the man. He still hadn't noticed her, so she first took a sip of the drink she'd picked up along the way before saying a word.

"Are you going to go talk to her or what?"

Xavier jumped and turned around quickly to face

Martine, almost spilling his drink. Blushing at getting caught, he cleared his throat. "I don't want to bother her right now."

"Probably a good choice. If you talking to her will make her mad, this isn't the place to do it."

"No, it's not. But I came early to look around. I'll be leaving shortly."

"Do you want me to say anything?"

"No. Let her have the evening. She deserves it, after all. I'll get in touch—which, by the way, I never found out how to do." He raised an eyebrow toward Martine.

"I don't have her number. But I can tell you where she is staying."

"Really? You would do that?"

"Look, I don't know what happened between the two of you. She mentioned your name a couple of times in the last few weeks, but not in a good way. I do know she is waiting to talk to you."

"Hmm. That is interesting. She knows how to get ahold of me, though."

"You were the one seeking her out."

"Okay. Where?"

"You know her property next door to the studio?"

"Yes." His eyes widened. "She's staying there?"

"Now you've got it."

"Was she there when I stopped by the shop?"

"Heavens, no. Well, I don't think so." Martine scratched her temple in thought. "Actually, she might have been. She showed up at the shop a day later, and I think she mentioned she was already in town at that time. I never put two and two together, but it would make sense, wouldn't it?"

Xavier shook his head. "Hiding out for years. What made her decide to have a showing now?" He waved his hand around.

"Honestly, I don't know. You'd have to ask her. I haven't talked to her much over the past several weeks, as I've been busy with my own sculpture. Her life is her own, as is mine. So, on that note, I'm going to continue to wander around, and you need to leave before she spots you."

"Will do. Thanks."

Martine walked away and eventually found someone else to converse with. She was introduced to a few others, and eventually the gossip mill realized who she was, which brought others around her to discuss her sculptures and the one that would be installed in the park.

Georgia and Gary visited with Xavier for a few moments, before he rushed out the door of the gallery. He wanted to make sure they didn't tell Charity he was there, and they promised, although reluctantly. Xavier had been over to their house many times in the past, accompanied by Charity. He would have been a great husband for her, and the couple were sorry to see things hadn't worked out. Georgia warned Charity, more than once, about how she was neglecting him and putting her career before everything else. When Xavier left town, Charity stated that the subject of their relationship was out of bounds.

Georgia caught him looking at Charity and wondered what he was thinking but believed they'd never gotten over each other. Neither one had had another long-term partner that she was aware of, either. This was going to be interesting, if and when, they ever got around to talking. She mentioned to him that Charity was waiting for him to make the first move. Nodding, he said he would, very soon, and mentioned that he'd told Martine the exact same thing just a few minutes earlier. Both Georgia and Gary ran a little interference to ensure that Xavier got out without Charity seeing him. But Georgia knew that when those two got together, there would be fireworks. And she didn't mean a fight, either.

Xavier waited until Charity was surrounded by several others, including Georgia and Gary, then finally managed to escape the gallery unnoticed. He hoped he wasn't in any of the pictures that were being taken. The media would have a heyday bringing up the past, and he was sure Charity wouldn't want their past relationship mentioned. He didn't either, as a matter of fact. Yet he couldn't help but admire how she looked. The dress suited her too. Her dark hair flowed around her face naturally, and, to Xavier, she appeared to not be enjoying the evening as she had in the past. There was definitely something different about her. He wasn't sure what it was, but something subtle. Now he was really anxious to talk to her. And to think she was right under his nose all this time. He shook his head. He couldn't believe it when Martine mentioned she was living next door, and she hadn't even realized Charity was there. Shaking his head again, he pulled into the hotel garage and went to the bar. He needed a drink and wanted to think about Charity undisturbed. Sitting at the end of the bar, his drink arrived at the same time as Buck. So much for being undisturbed.

***

As the night progressed, Charity's smile became more forced. She finally sought out Martine and they went to Mr. Piedmont's office to get out of the limelight for a few minutes. They sat down on a comfy couch and took off their shoes. Both let out groans of agony as they rubbed their feet.

"I forgot to not wear new shoes to these things. Man, my feet are killing me." Charity sat back and stretched her legs out in front of her, wiggling her feet around to get the circulation going again.

"Mine too." Martine mimicked Charity's pose for a moment before sitting back up suddenly. "Oh. I forgot to tell you—I met Mr. Charles Higgens tonight. Mr. Parker showed him my drawing for the park statue, and he wants to commission something for his gardens."

Charity had closed her eyes but opened them again at the mention of Mr. Higgens's name. Pulling herself into a sitting position, she replied, "Wow. That's a coup. They have lovely gardens. I've only seen them once and that was for just a brief moment. Let me see, if I remember right, his wife died a couple of years ago."

"You're right." Martine struggled to put her shoes back on. "He mentioned that he wanted something that represented her, since she loved her gardens. I guess she spent a lot of time out there while she was sick."

"What did you tell him?"

"I told him I needed to spend some time walking around them, of course." She chuckled. "I need the muse." They both laughed. "All right. I confess I wanted to get a good look at them, but I truly do need to see them in order to make something that will honor his wife. I told him I wouldn't make one that looked like her. It had to be something that would blend in well with the garden. I think he was a little miffed, but I explained that portraits and photos captured the true essence of his wife, not a sculpture. I'm not Michelangelo, you know."

"I'm sure whatever you come up with will be perfect." Charity put on her shoes, too, and got up. "Okay. I'm ready. Thanks for taking a break with me. We only have about another hour to go."

"Thank heavens. I don't know how you did these all the time."

"Me neither, but I know it wasn't wearing new shoes." They were laughing as they went out the door and ran right into Mr. Piedmont.

"There you are. I have latecomers looking for you. All I said was that you needed the ladies' room for a minute."

"Close enough. I hope you are doing your job and selling everything."

Mr. Piedmont looked miffed, and said, "Don't you worry about my job. You go finish doing yours." He tapped his watch. "We are almost at the witching hour."

Charity smirked and nodded her head. The women went back into the throng. Thankfully, it had thinned out some. Martine was soon finding her way around the room, letting Charity have the full attention she deserved. Over an hour later, the last of the guests were ushered out of the building. Charity and Martine thanked Mr. Piedmont for the successful night as they waited for the limo to be brought around for them. He promised to call Charity the following afternoon with the numbers. During her renovations, she moved the shop's phoneline over to her loft, found an inexpensive updated model, and now had a local number for people to call and leave messages. The two kicked their shoes off immediately upon settling into the limo. They laid their heads back and relaxed, seldom talking. It seemed that talking was all Charity did all night, and she was exhausted. Thanking the driver, the women parted ways, and both of them were ready to get into some comfy pajamas and go to bed.

Sleeping late, Charity awakened to bright sun shining through the newly installed skylights. Last evening, she lay looking at the stars shining brightly above her, and gradually fell into a deep sleep. The skylight had been a great idea, one which Charity quickly approved of and thoroughly enjoyed. With her blackout curtains, she didn't get to enjoy the sunlight. The problem was there was no privacy with them open. Someday, she hoped to replace the loft windows with ones similar to those she put in the front door. Then she wouldn't even have to have curtains if she didn't want to.

Lounging around the apartment that afternoon, she was almost asleep in her recliner when the phone rang. Startled, her heart sped up and Charity jerked into a sitting position. Grabbing the phone on the third ring, she was happy to see it was Mr. Piedmont.

"Mr. Piedmont. What is the good word of the day?"

"Oh, my lovely. The good word of the day is that every piece sold. Every piece. What do you think of that?"

She was wide awake upon that news. "Are you sure?"

"I needed to take care of a couple of calls this morning, but we have confirmed the purchase of every piece. Even the smallest ones flew out the door."

"That is great. I'm relieved too."

"So, darling, I want to arrange to have more of your pieces brought in on display."

"I'm not going through that ordeal again. You can have a show without me."

"No, no, no. You misunderstand me. I mean, I want to bring the rest of your inventory over here to display at all times. We will put out a token few and add and change out routinely. I expect that the rest of your supply will diminish rapidly."

"They could have come to the shop, you know."

"Pish posh. What drivel. You know they need to shop where they will be seen and talked about. Not in a shoddy neighborhood like yours. Sorry. I don't mean to upset you, but you know I'm right. These are not the type of people to lower themselves to your neighborhood."

Charity sighed. "I know. Except I live here. Don't they realize that?"

"Oh, I'm sure they know you have a studio there, but live there? Ha. I'm betting they think you live in a penthouse on the north side or something. Not that anyone asked me, and I'm not telling."

"Let's not bring it up until after you sell all my inventory, then."

"Yes. Let's not. Ta-da, darling. I will talk to you soon."

She heard the dial tone, so Charity hung up slowly. Smiling, she kicked back in her recliner and thought about the nice, fat check that Mr. Piedmont would be handing her soon. Closing her eyes, she was able to nap easily, knowing she was financially solvent once again.

***

Now that Xavier's peaceful drink ended up to be anything but, he went to his room and began packing. He would have to leave first thing in the morning to handle some problems at another site and would probably be gone for some time. In the meantime, he would leave Buck in charge to handle any problems that arose trying to get permits for the new housing development. The mayor was on board, but there were many hoops to go through, including changing the area from industrial and commercial to residential. Otherwise, his company wasn't going to receive a tax break for all this work, and the plans would go down the tubes. Calling the front desk, he notified them of his early morning checkout, then prepared for another restless night. He hadn't slept well since coming to town and was unable to find Charity. Now that he knew she was staying in town, he was trying to get up the nerve to talk to her but had gotten cold feet once he saw her at the gallery. Morning arrived and Xavier was headed out of town once again. Charity's property dilemma was going to have to wait until he returned.

***

A month had gone by, and Mr. Piedmont had finally removed the last of Charity's pieces to the gallery. She also talked the men into moving the showcases to the back room out of the way. She and Martine had tried, but without the proper equipment they gave up quickly. Now the space was wide open, and you could see what terrible shape the floor and walls were in. Mr. Piedmont was ready to leave the old shop now that he knew for sure Charity wasn't holding back any items.

"Charity, my love, I have had so many calls after your showing that I'm sure the rest won't take long to sell. You need to think about making more of your shiny trinkets."

"Mr. Piedmont, I prefer to call my masterpieces shiny baubles." They looked at each other silently, then both burst out laughing.

Wiping tears from his face, Mr. Piedmont jerked his vest down and straightened his shoulders. "Not too many people can get me laughing like you, my dear."

"It's a talent." She shook her head. "I haven't made anything in years, and still don't have an idea forthcoming. If I do, you will be the first to know. After all, I can buy groceries now."

He shook his head. "I know darn well that Gary and Georgia have probably got a wonderful financial package built for you. I can't imagine they would let you fritter away all your money."

"Of course, you're right again, Mr. Piedmont. But a girl has to have some spending money, you know."

"I know." He rubbed his hands together. "I need to get back and set up a small display for you. Then I will be making a few calls. People are waiting, and I will tell them these are the last of your stash. Makes people greedy, you know."

Charity reached over and gave him a hug. The old codger loved talking people out of their money. Of course, he received a nice percentage for his commission. "Call me sometime. I will await my next check with bated breath."

Mr. Piedmont returned the hug, gave her a kiss on the cheek, and was out the door, leaving the dusty floor blowing behind him.

***

Grabbing a broom, the dirt was soon swept into a pile. She didn't hear Martine walk into the room. "Wow. This looks way different."

Charity jumped and put her hand over her heart. "Oh. You scared me. I must have been deep in thought over all this dirt."

"Sorry. I was going upstairs for a snack. Feel like

joining me?"

"Sure. You have something I can put this dirt in?"

Martine grabbed a wastebasket from the back room. "This pile of dirt makes it look like I never swept the place."

"It didn't help with the men coming in and out. And we certainly couldn't get under the showcases all these years. But now that the place is empty, it certainly shows how much work it needs."

Taking a good look around, Martine frowned. "Wow. This place needs an upgrade."

Charity laughed. "Yes, it does. And I have plenty of time on my hands. Let's get that snack. I've suddenly decided I'm starved."

The two women sat for the next hour or so, catching up on life in general, and talking about renovating the old showroom. They decided instead of a snack they would make a meal, and the two talked over their preparations. Martine's BBQ set was up on the small balcony, so they whipped up some steaks and baked potatoes. By the time they were conversing over coffee the evening was turning cool, and they needed to go back inside. Both having enjoyed the evening, they agreed to get together soon.

Charity walked back to her place, and Martine went back to her workshop. She stood and looked at the statue. Almost completed, she hoped to have Charity look at it before the man who commissioned it, Mr. Parker, came over. With her critical eye, she felt that Charity would be able to see something she may have missed. This piece would set her up financially for the rest of the year, and she wanted to make sure it was going to be worth the man's money. The spot was prepared and waiting for the statue's arrival. She hoped Mr. Parker and the community would be very happy.

Her plan was to take a few days of rest after she completed the statue. Then she would head over to Mr. Higgens's place to check out the gardens once again. Her first trip was spent listening to him talk about his wife and how she loved the gardens. Still too early in the year to be in full bloom, she promised to come back and walk through again. She was sure the place would be much more beautiful the second time.

Martine wasn't disappointed in the gardens. A week after the installation and unveiling of the statue in the park, she drove over, and Mr. Higgens let her walk through the garden to try and visualize what would be appropriate. Sketch pad in hand, she meandered around, sat on a bench to take in her surroundings, and breathed in the fragrant air. Finally, Martine began sketching page after page, drawing several options for Mr. Higgens to choose from. It was close to three hours later before she opened the patio doors and called his name. Sitting on the patio in the shade with a glass of iced tea in front of them, they talked about each sketch and what Martine felt it represented. It took only a moment before the last sketch drew him in.

"This one. You don't even need to explain it to me."

"You're sure?"

"Yes. This is the essence of my wife, right here. I can see her nod and approve of this." He turned his teary eyes up toward Martine. "Yes. Definitely this one."

"Very good. This one it is. Now, this will take several months. I will eventually give you the size of the base I need when I know for sure."

"We have that worn out gazebo in the center of the main garden. My wife made me promise I would remove it after she was gone. Would that spot work?"

"That would be a lovely place. But you don't want to replace the gazebo?"

"No. My wife loved it out there, and it holds too many memories for me. Since it needs torn down anyway, we can put the cement pad to good use."

"Okay. You make sure the cement can hold the statue without cracking. I'm not sure the pad will be strong enough because of its age."

"I'll take care of replacing it after I tear down the gazebo. If I'm not mistaken, it already has some cracks in the base. By the time you are ready, it will be cured and ready for you. Let me go inside and get my checkbook to give you the down payment."

***

When Martine left, check in hand, she was almost crying. The sketch Mr. Higgens picked out was her favorite, and she felt like Mrs. Higgens was guiding her hand as she worked on highlighting roses and other flowers into her drawing. She had no idea what the names of all those flowers were, but it didn't matter. What mattered was that it was the perfect drawing. She spent much more time with details, feeling Mrs. Higgens right there with her. With Mr. Parker's check already in the bank, Martine decided this check was going right into her savings. She was delighted that there would be one to match when the statue was done. The money was going to come in very handy to set her up for her future.

4

When Buck found Xavier in the bar after the gallery opening, he couldn't decide if he was more upset at not being alone to fret over Cassidy, or that there were problems in St. Louis that cropped up. While packing, he spent less and less time thinking of the problem dealing with Cassidy and more on what was in store for him when his flight landed in St. Louis. Buck had done all he could to stave off the zoning office until Xavier met with them. Here they were in the middle of a huge housing project, and suddenly the zoning office decided to pull the plug. With a hundred and fifty apartments in different stages of development, there was no time to waste. The construction crew already broke ground on the next building, and now they were at a standstill. A few late-night phone calls later, Xavier would be meeting his company lawyers at the airport in St. Louis, where they would then head straight for the zoning office in question. Needless to say, he got very little sleep that night, and wondered why he didn't just take a late night flight in the first place.

Once in St. Louis, he checked the board and knew he still had a couple of hours to wait for his lawyers to arrive. He found his way to a vendor for breakfast and sat back to do some work. He sent a message to his lawyers to let them know where he would be waiting. Two and a half hours later, the three men made their way to the rental car that Xavier had secured at the last minute. He decided to drive to the site instead of renting a rideshare. After all, he was probably going to be in town for some time. The GPS took them directly to the building site first, where they found the contractor in his trailer, sitting behind his desk with his feet up. Pete jumped up when they walked inside.

"Xavier. Man, am I glad to see you. This is a disaster. I have guys just sitting around waiting for word. Are we working or not?"

"I don't know," Xavier said as they shook hands. "You remember Ken and Gene, my corporate lawyers?"

"Sure. Glad you're here. What's the next step?"

"We needed to know what they told you exactly. Do you have a paper that says to stop, or was this just verbally done?"

Pete dug around on his desk and pulled out a letter from under the blueprints. "They brought this over and demanded we stop immediately. Not that they can stop us from finishing the first building, but something is fishy here. We have all the permits and paperwork that was issued. I don't know why it all came to a screeching halt."

Ken stepped forward and patted Pete's shoulder. "Let's see all the correspondence related to this project. We need to take a quick look before heading to the zoning office."

The men took copies of everything, and when they were satisfied that all was in order, they were ready to go butt heads with someone. As the men talked during the tedious trip to the zoning office, they wondered if someone's palm hadn't been greased, making waves. With no knowledge of what happened, they were in the dark. Finally finding a place to park, the men went into the office armed to the teeth and ready for a fight. The secretary stopped them in their tracks.

"You do not have an appointment until three this afternoon. I can't possibly get you in earlier than that."

Xavier sighed. "I realize that, but we were hoping to get these issues worked out long before then."

"You might as well go have lunch. Mr. Bertrum won't be back in his office until just before your meeting." The three men gave each other a look and decided they might as well leave. "There is a nice restaurant just down the street on your left."

"Thank you," Xavier grumbled. "We'll be back for our appointment."

As the men walked toward the restaurant, Xavier apologized for bullying his way into the office. Of course he had an appointment. Shaking his head, he knew that making a scene was no way to get into anyone's good graces. He would apologize again to the secretary when they returned. Just because he had a lousy night's sleep didn't mean he should take it out on an innocent bystander.

With a late lunch and a drink to settle his nerves, the men walked back to wait until their appointment time. Xavier apologized to the secretary right away, and asked if they could sit in the waiting room until their appointment time. With the crazy traffic, there was no way they could go anywhere and return in a short amount of time. Each one quietly worked on their laptops or phones, seldom saying anything. The secretary continued her job, and for the most part ignored the men. Ten minutes after three, the men were taken to Mr. Bertram's office.

After introductions, Mr. Bertrum said, "Have a seat, gentlemen. Sorry I was a little late for our appointment. Let's see, we are here to discuss the problems with the Goldenflower addition, correct?"

"Correct. We have all the correct building permits, and the zoning ordinances were legally changed. We don't understand the issue in continuing our project. The men were breaking ground for the second building when someone stopped by to halt construction. You can understand our dismay at this turn of events."

"Yes. Well, an issue has come up. The previous owner has filed a petition to stop the construction, stating that they were not told what the land was to be used for and didn't agree to it being torn up for apartment buildings."

The men looked at each other in dismay. Ken leaned toward Mr. Bertrum. "Excuse me? The previous owner? How does that affect us currently? Mr. Thomas has owned that land for over a year, and we did all our due diligence to make sure it was zoned properly before we ever surveyed the area."

"Yes, hmm." Mr. Bertrum shuffled some papers on his desk. "All I know is that there is a stop order in place, and we have to honor that at this time."

Xavier frowned. "What does the zoning board have to do with it now?"

"We got involved because the previous owners have stated we changed the zoning without his approval."

Ken scoffed. "This is outrageous. Legally, the previous owner has no legal right to stop anything."

"As it stands, we are all stuck. This will have to play out in the court of law now."

"Can we finish the current building, or does that stop too?"

"I wouldn't do anything at this point. If you spend money finishing the apartments and the previous owner wins, you could be out a fortune."

"This is bizarre. Who do we need to talk to next?"

"I don't know when the court hearing is yet. I doubt it's scheduled. And as late as it's getting today, you won't get to the courthouse in time to talk to anyone."

Xavier stood up, anger boiling over. Gritting his teeth, he thanked Mr. Bertrum, and he and his lawyers left the office building. They made their way to the car and got inside before Xavier exploded.

"Of all the nerve! I can't believe anyone in their right mind would allow the halt order to go through."

Gene hadn't said much and spent a lot of his time scrolling on his phone. "I've been researching this guy. Not Bertrum, the previous owner. Name is Calhoun. I think he has a judge or two in his pocket. Looks like he's done this before in a different county, and the new owners paid him off big time for him to drop the case. We need to make sure we get an impartial judge assigned to this case right away."

Ken laughed. "A judge or two, huh? I'd say we could probably handle a crooked judge. I know a few judges of my own around here."

Xavier and Gene both stared at Ken and said at the same time, "You do?"

"Yeah. I have cousins and aunts and uncles here, so I'll make some calls this evening. Now, where is our hotel?"

Blowing out a deep breath, Xavier said, "I don't know. Where do you want it to be?"

Gene said he already had one picked out, and the address was typed into the GPS. Xavier called Pete and told him to keep the finishing crew working on the apartments but send the construction crew home for the next week. He hoped by then they would have an idea how long this whole debacle would last. When push came to shove, Ken and Gene could hold their own against the very best. That's why Xavier paid them the big bucks.

After handling some business, which included a visit to the courthouse, there was nothing left for Xavier to do but wait. It only took a couple of days before he was bored and stir-crazy, so he kept pestering his lawyers. Gene took him to the airport and sent him back to the home office in Oakville. At least he could keep busy there instead of being in the lawyers' way all the time. Buck was still in Churchtown, and Xavier wasn't ready to go back and face Charity quite yet.

Rainy kept Xavier busy for the next several days. He also set up visits in other areas of the country where he might be able to expand his holdings. A few trips here and there led to nothing, but he was busy. Gene and Ken had everything handled in St. Louis, and he would be flying back for the court hearing. Ken sent him an encouraging message the day before and hoped that meant they would be back up and running soon at the construction site. The men had been stalled for days on end, and it was costing Xavier a fortune. He sent everyone home while they waited for a decision.

After three weeks, the preliminary hearing was finally scheduled. Gene managed to have a new judge assigned to handle the case. He made sure that the original judge was disqualified due to a conflict of interest, the conflict being the judge was golfing buddies with the complainant. Point one to Gene. Not only that, but the original court date was also stretched out to almost a year later. The current judge was willing to get it on his docket immediately. Point two, Ken. Xavier probably didn't need to be at the hearing, but he wanted to face the previous owner and make sure the guy knew they weren't messing around.

The flight didn't get into St. Louis early enough for Xavier to visit with his lawyers in person before the hearing started and promised to meet them at the courthouse. He barely made it in time, getting to his chair just in time to stand up for the judge to enter. As the hearing started, Xavier looked over at the other table. The lawyer smirked, and the previous owner tried to act nonchalant. He certainly hoped Gene and Ken had time to do all their homework on those two.

Mr. Calhoun's lawyer explained his case to the judge and managed to make Xavier's company look like they were sneaking thieves. Xavier cringed at some of the things the lawyer mentioned and wondered if his company really looked that bad to others. Several minutes later, it was their turn to make their case, and it was finally time for Ken to present their defense.

"Your Honor, thank you for scheduling this hearing so quickly. I have a few things I want to bring up that our esteemed lawyer sitting at the other table may have forgotten to mention. First of all, Judge Cannon had to be recused due to his personal relationship with Mr. Calhoun. Now, Judge Cannon has held court for Mr. Calhoun on other occasions for this same exact reason and has always ruled in favor for Mr. Calhoun."

Xavier looked over at Mr. Calhoun and saw that both he and his lawyer turned ashen over that revelation. Under his breath, he said, "Whoa."

Ken continued. "Now. All of the paperwork we completed ahead of breaking ground is above board and completed to local regulations. I contend that Mr. Calhoun has no right to ask that work be stopped and that this issue should not even have come in front of a judge. I ask that all fees be charged back to Mr. Calhoun. And, for good measure, I would ask that his lawyer and Judge Cannon be investigated for unethical conduct. Thank you,

Your Honor." Ken sat back down and didn't even glance at the other table.

The judge looked at Mr. Calhoun and his lawyer. "Do you have anything else to say before I make my ruling?"

Mr. Calhoun whispered to his lawyer and there ensued a quiet argument. The lawyer finally stood up and announced, "No, Your Honor. We are withdrawing the case."

"I see. Stay where you are for a moment. Mr. Thomas, I am dismissing this case and you are all free to leave and complete the work you have started for our great city. I will be issuing a judgement back to Mr. Calhoun to pay the expenses for this debacle. Please send the court your bill."

"Thank you, Your Honor." The three men hurriedly left and could hear the judge reprimand the other two as the door closed behind them. Xavier turned to his men. "Wow. When you said you had something good on those guys, I can't believe you two came up with all of that information."

Ken shrugged. "Gene here is a great sleuth. All I needed to do was bring up the truth. They knew we had them dead to rights. I have a feeling Judge Cannon is going to be feeling some heat shortly. Gene made sure the media was sitting in the courtroom, and they won't let that little nugget go to waste."

Xavier cracked up laughing. "You two." He shook his head. "Let's go home. I'll call Pete on our way to pick up your stuff at the hotel."

"You got it, boss."

Gene slid behind the wheel of the car. Xavier made the promised call to Pete and proceeded to make reservations for their return trip. Actually, he called Rainy to make them, but that was beside the point. They had time for a celebratory meal before heading to the airport, and for the first time in a few weeks, Xavier felt relieved that something had finally gone right. Briefly, he thought about Charity but pushed her out of his mind as they began discussing baseball.

Back in Oakville, Xavier sat back in his chair and twirled his pen while daydreaming. He had been in meetings most of the day, finalizing paperwork on several projects. Buck finished his work in Churchtown, and all that was left was talking to Charity. He had been gone for almost three months now, and it was way past time for him to return. Always finding a reason to go elsewhere, he was running out of excuses. Mayor Spears led the charge to change the area from commercial to residential, and a letter would have gone out to Charity to see if she wanted to contest the issue. Buck mentioned, upon his return to the office, that Charity had not offered any complaints to the zoning change and didn't even go to the meeting. Suspicious at heart, Xavier wondered what that meant. After all, she had a gallery there, didn't she? But maybe she was gone again. He was afraid to ask Buck, and the conversation soon led to projects elsewhere.

With no further catastrophes to handle, Rainy booked Xavier a flight to Churchtown. It was time to face up to his fears. He'd chickened out before, and he might do so once again. He wasn't sure if he would ever be up to talking to her. They were both angry when they broke up, and once he moved his headquarters out of town to Oakville, they never ran across each other's paths again. After all these years, he thought they may be able to have a civil conversation at some point. There was no time like the present to see if that could or would happen. Landing late that evening, he made his way to the hotel, threw his suitcase on the bed, and stared out the window at all the bright lights. He was home, and the thought caused a pang of loneliness to come over him. Lost in thought, it was quite some time before he prepared for bed. He lay there looking at the ceiling, the lights from the city blinking and wavering in front of him. The last thought he had before falling asleep was of Charity.

5

Seldom did actual mail arrive for Charity, but one day Martine received a certified letter. She heard knocking and almost didn't go see who it was. The mailman was walking back to his truck by the time she realized it might be important. She yelled out the door, and the mailman brought it back to her. She signed it and thanked the man. He was grumpy, given the slow response from Martine, but she just smiled and closed the door. Since Charity was working almost every day in the building, she laid the envelope on a paint can and went back to work.

Charity didn't enter the old shop for a couple of days. She was recovering from all the stretching and climbing on the ladder while cutting in the paint around the ceiling. The area was extremely high, and she needed scaffolding if she was going to do that safely. She found a company to rent from, and the store brought it out and set it up for her. Frowning, she wondered why she hadn't thought of that in the first place. Walking over to her paint cans, she noticed the envelope. Seeing that Martine signed for the certified mail, she tore it open.

Finding a stool to sit on, Charity reread the papers a couple of times. Sighing, she sat with her back to the wall and closed her eyes. The city was going to change her property designation to residential unless she complained and showed a reason why her two properties should be exceptions. A few months ago, she would have had a fit.

She opened her eyes and looked around. There was no shop to worry about now. Charity figured that Martine's work area wouldn't matter to anyone. After all, if someone had a workshop in their garage or basement no one cared. She threw the papers on the floor and organized her paints and brushes on the scaffolding. She climbed onto the platform and pushed a button. Grinning, the whole thing raised up to exactly where she needed to be. Looking down, she felt much safer than on a ladder. As she painted, her thoughts drifted to the varying changes, and decided not to worry about them. No one, especially Xavier, had talked to her about selling yet, so that was a good thing. Maybe her plan to expand the living space in both buildings would work out after all.

Martine watched as Charity lowered the scaffolding so she could get down. "Wow. That's quite the contraption."

"Isn't it though? Makes my life so much easier. What do you think of the color so far?"

"It's the same as outside, isn't it?"

"Yeah. The color is light enough, so I figured to do this whole room in it. Then I need to put down a new floor. What do you think? Hardwood or carpeting?"

"Hmm. Depends. What are you thinking this room should be?"

"I don't know. A living room, family room, or some place for entertainment maybe."

"Certainly hardwood if you consider spills and such. A big soft throw rug in the middle would soften the look."

"Good idea. After I get the painting done, the curtains I'm having made for the front window should be ready to hang. I wanted the same color as the trim on the outside, so I needed to special-order to match. Besides, after all the work I'm going through to improve the looks of the place, I want it to be comfortable."

Martine chuckled. "I would have just hung up a blanket or something to get me by."

"Nope. We do this the right way. This place will look fabulous when I'm done."

"It already looks better. You sure you don't want any help?"

"I'm good. You continue working on your own project. The more I see this place coming together, the more excited I am about getting this scaffolding over to the other building to do the same thing. In fact, I've already ordered the curtains."

"Well, I'll leave you to it then. I need to go see my mother this evening."

"See you later."

Cleaning up, Charity picked up her papers and tucked them in her pocket. She would review them again over supper, just to make sure there wasn't a hidden agenda she may have missed. Turning back before locking the door, she smiled at the paint job. Once she'd got her scaffolding, she'd repaired several mistakes she made earlier while working from the ladder. Locking up, she took a breath of fresh air before walking slowly back to her building. The spring weather was refreshing, but she knew summer would be hitting soon. Charity made her way to her shower first thing, then took her supper out to the patio. She put her feet up and relaxed as the sunlight began to fade. Picking up her papers once again, she perused them and found nothing alarming. Charity would take them to Gary and Georgia's tomorrow and have them look over the paperwork, noting a fresh set of eyes wouldn't hurt. She hoped that Maurice would be making her a special dessert again. That man was a saint.

The weeks were sliding by, and Charity had all but finished her painting and repairs on both buildings. The new flooring was completed in Martine's building, and the workers would return to finish in her building later in the day. The drapes were beautiful against the coloring on the walls, and she was pleased with her decision to stay with the same colors as the outside. The tone was so muted that it softened the large space. Waiting on the furniture delivery made her impatient, but she also couldn't wait to have the two spaces finished. Hearing the truck pull up outside had her scrambling to run down to the door to let the men inside to finish the floor. Just a few odds and ends were needed to finish, so Charity sat in the stairwell and watched the men as they quickly finished the job and gathered up their tools.

"I'm sorry we couldn't get this finished yesterday. I guess we didn't account for as much waste when trimming pieces."

"No problem. I'm just glad that the company still had an extra box or two."

The foreman laughed. "I think they are used to us shorting ourselves. We try not to waste anything, but now we have about a half a box we can leave with you to save for repairs if needed."

"Perfect. You can put that in the back room where you saved those other pieces."

On his way out the door, the man turned. "I just want to thank you for selecting my company to lay these floors. The space turned out really spectacular, and I'm jealous."

Charity laughed and looked around the open space. "It certainly did turn out that way. You guys did a great job. When I decide to replace the flooring in the lofts, I'll give you a call."

"Appreciate it. Thanks again." He tipped his hat before walking out the door.

She found herself looking around again before climbing the steps to the loft. Charity stopped halfway up and looked down at the space. The furniture would arrive in a couple of days. She couldn't wait to see the finished project. As she went inside the apartment, Charity stopped suddenly, then turned around and glanced back downstairs. Smiling, she turned back to the apartment and went to her desk. Once situated, she dug out some drawing paper, a fresh pencil, and went to work. Before she knew it, an hour had gone by. But a thrill went through her as she realized that her drawing was the first glimpse of a new art piece. And it wasn't anything like she had done before. Excitement built up inside of her as she stared at her drawing. If she actually managed to put it together, this piece could be the starting point of a new direction in her life.

The following day, Charity began boxing up her supplies in the back room of her old studio. She planned to make a new workshop in her own back room and leave Martine to her space. That way, no one would be disturbed at any time. Besides, she didn't want any witnesses if what she created became a disaster. It took several trips back and forth, but Charity finally had everything moved. It was nice that Martine had been gone all morning too, as she didn't want to intrude on her space, time, or make her feel like she needed to help.

Before leaving the building on her last trip, she lowered the full box of supplies on her old desk before walking over to the sculpture that stood in the middle of the floor. She hadn't paid much attention to it before, but Martine was outdoing herself with this one. Charity could tell that this sculpture, in particular, had heart and soul built into it. Mr. Higgens was going to be more than pleased, she was sure. Finding a piece of scratch paper, Charity wrote a quick note about being impressed with her current work in progress, then propped it on Martine's desk for her to find easily. She added a quick mention about taking her supplies next door, just so Martine wouldn't worry about where everything had gone. Picking up her box, she headed out to her new workshop.

Looking around, Charity would have to do something about ordering a new worktable and better lighting.

Nothing she had was suitable, and what was in the old workshop was secured tightly. Besides, it was time for an upgrade. If she was going to go back to creating art, she needed to do this right. Calling her distributer, they were surprised to hear from her after all those years after she disappeared. More than willing to provide whatever Charity wanted, they emailed a new catalog for her to peruse. That evening, she spent several hours going through and picking out items, crossing some off, only to restart her list. By the time the screen was blurring in front of her, Charity finalized her list and sent it off to the distributer. She giggled and clapped her hands in glee, then promptly felt silly. Crawling into bed, she was still smiling as she dropped off to sleep.

The next few days were spent setting up the new living spaces in both buildings. Martine was just as excited and helped Charity move the furniture around until they were both satisfied. With a large rug in the center, seating on three sides, and a large coffee table, the place was finally coming together. Charity was going to allow Martine to decorate the rest as she pleased. With one last request from Martine, Charity finally agreed to an increase in the rent to offset her living in the loft. All of the utilities would be transferred into Martine's name the following month. Then Martine followed Charity to her place, to organize her furniture next. Similar in style and elegance, it didn't take as long to put everything in place. Finishing, they flopped down on the couch to relax.

"I see you took most of your things from the workshop. Did you finally decide to get back to work?"

Charity nodded. "I think all of this decorating finally opened up the block on my creativity. But, instead of all of that abstract glasswork like I'd been doing, I'm going to try my hand at stained glass and pieces that will reflect beauty and color. But right now, the pieces will only be for me. I don't know if I'm ready to create for the public again. Not to change the subject, but I need you to know that what you have done with your current project is stunning, and I can't wait to hear what Mr. Higgens thinks about it. You have inspired me, Martine."

"Oh, my. Thank you for the compliment. Coming from you, that means more to me than you can imagine."

"I mean it. The piece you made for the park was stunning, but this one is alive. I can only hope to create something that speaks to me like that piece does, and you aren't even finished with it yet."

"I have a lot of work left. I can't believe you can see that already. This piece means a lot to me, more than any other I've done. I can't explain it, exactly, but I think Mrs. Higgens is guiding me through this process." She shook her head. "It's weird, I know."

"No, not really. As artists, we feel things that others don't."

Martine stood up. "I need to get back home. I've enjoyed our visits and helping you arrange furniture, but we both know I need to get back to work. Or at least go home."

Giving each other a hug first, Martine went back to her workshop and stood looking at her sculpture. She was glad that Charity could already feel its warmth and soul. It gave her hope that she was well on the way to making her most memorable sculpture. Deciding to rest instead of work, she went back to her apartment. Tomorrow would be soon enough to continue working.

6

The trip to Churchtown went by quickly. Xavier could have driven, but he was used to making the trip by plane. Renting his car, he decided to take a detour to the other side of town, where he grew up. He hadn't been back in the old neighborhood since his parents moved to Florida. Pulling up across the street from the house where he grew up, he sat and stared at the peeling paint. The new owners hadn't changed a thing, nor had they given any thought to taking care of the outside. Maybe they couldn't afford to; he didn't know. Looking around the neighborhood, the homes were all beginning to show their age, and it made him want to repair them all.

Churchtown was settled by a handful of immigrants from different countries and cultures. Each group built their own church once their neighborhoods were established. A traveler going through commented on the number of churches and steeples they could see from miles away. The community decided to stick with the obvious, and Churchtown became their official name. Although many of the old neighborhoods were long gone, you could still find an original church or two in the area.

Xavier had grown up in a lower-middle-class family. His father worked hard in a factory, and his mother cared for him and his sister when they were little, only going to work in the library after they were both in school. When Xavier made his first millions from an investment he made on a dare, he talked his parents into retiring and living wherever they chose. They traveled all over, and, despite believing they would never leave their old home, they stumbled upon a community of younger retirees in Florida and fell in love with the area. Xavier bought a group of condos as an investment and moved his parents to their dream home. With no yardwork to do, no job to go to, no family to worry over, his parents were living their best life when they chose their new lifestyle. Now, his sister and her family would drive down to see them couple of times a year. One of the condos was kept as a short-term rental, which allowed his sister and family to always have a comfortable place to stay. Xavier would stop by whenever he was nearby and made sure his parents never needed anything.

His daydreaming state was jerked to reality when a couple of young kids came screeching to a halt on their bikes in front of the house. Smiling, he watched as they roughed and tumbled in the yard before tearing into the house. It did his heart good to see the boys enjoying themselves on his old stomping grounds as much as he had at that age. Putting the car in gear, he slowly pulled out and headed toward Charity's. It was time to stop putting off the inevitable. If he was going to be working practically right next door to her, they needed to find a way to get along. Buck handled all the groundwork, and in a just a few days the first block was due to be completely demolished. A crew was already there to get started. The pigeons had no idea what was going to happen to their homes. Xavier shook his head when Buck told him that he had someone going over ahead of time to make sure there weren't any baby pigeons or eggs in nests that would be harmed during the destruction of the old buildings.

Delaying his stop in front of Charity's, Xavier drove around the four blocks and checked everything over once again. Still satisfied with their final decisions, he pulled up in front of the building where Martine said Charity was living. He didn't know if she was still there or not after all this time. As he sat there, it took him a minute to figure out what changed. Then he realized that the buildings sported upgraded siding and Charity's Shoppe sign was gone. Although the sun was going down, he was mesmerized by the changes that had been made since he'd been there three or four months previous. He could see a light on in the loft where Martine was staying, but no lights were visible in Charity's place. He took a deep breath and headed for the door. After a few knocks and waiting, he was hoping that she wasn't home rather than ignoring him. Knocking a couple more times, he walked around the outside of the building and didn't see any lights at all. He wondered if she had moved on by now. Almost relieved, he went back to the car and headed toward the hotel. Tomorrow, he would look for an apartment. Whenever he had extremely large projects like this, he would hang around for several months until he could be sure things were running smoothly. He and Buck often shared a place, and that would be what they planned for this time too.

After supper, Xavier looked through his phone to find Charity's Shoppe number to call and leave a message. Or maybe Martine was still answering. Either way, he wanted to set up an appointment to see her. If he hadn't heard back in a couple of days, he would stop by Georgia's place and see if they knew where she was. He had a feeling Georgia wanted them to talk and get things out in the open. It was too bad the mess in St. Louis came up first, because he should have handled it right after her showing at the gallery. The phone rang a couple of times and then went to voicemail. He left a message, then hung up quickly. Listening to Charity's voice took him back a decade when all he wanted was to hear her voice and have her talk to him. Almost shaking, he went downstairs to the bar to wait for Buck, who was arriving later that evening. They had a lot to do in the next few weeks, and fretting over Charity was taking up too much headspace.

By the time Buck arrived and visited for a few minutes, the men were both ready to call it a night. With the following day filled with errands, they were soon settled into their rooms. Tomorrow, Xavier was going to see a realtor and locate an apartment, while Buck was heading to a meeting with Mayor Spears and other members of the city council so they could finally sign off on the completed plans. Tearing down the old beat-up buildings wasn't the issue. What they planned to build in its place was, and so far Mayor Spears had been on their side. Buck could charm a rattlesnake, so Xavier wasn't worried.

The next afternoon, Xavier was just finalizing a short-term lease on an apartment when his phone rang. He almost didn't look at it, but once he glanced at the number, he realized it was Charity. Or so he hoped.

"Excuse me. I have to take this." He scribbled his name on the lease, stood up quickly, and, as he walked out into the hallway, answered his phone. "Hello?"

"Xavier. It's Charity."

He let out the breath he didn't realize he was holding. "Thank you for calling me back. I stopped by last night, but you didn't answer the door. I wondered if you were in town or not. I'd like to stop by and talk to you for a few minutes."

"I was out with friends last evening. The answer is yes, I'm in town, and yes, you can stop to talk to me. I'll be at my place the rest of the day."

"Great. How about five? Would that work?"

"Sure. I'll see you then."

Charity hung up and Xavier looked at his phone. He didn't realize his palms were sweating until then, so he wiped them off before going back into the apartment complex's office. He finished the formalities, picked up the keys, and headed for his car. He didn't know why he kept calling it an apartment, as it was more like a business suite. Everything he and Buck needed was available. The complex had one unit that was only rented to businessmen and charged an arm and a leg too. But it would be more comfortable than a hotel, plus it offered more privacy. If he needed to have meetings with the crew, he could book a small conference room. Calling Buck, he gave him the address. In the meantime, Xavier went back to the hotel and checked out. By the time both he and Buck unpacked in their new place, it was time for him to meet up with Charity. The men would have supper later and talk about how Buck's meetings went.

The traffic was terrible once again, so Xavier got off the main highway and took a back way. He arrived shortly after five and hoped that didn't mean they would start off on the wrong foot. As he walked up to the front door, he realized Charity was already there, waiting for him. Her dark hair billowed around her face, and her fair skin was more beautiful than he remembered. She had changed little over the years, except to become more attractive. He was sure his appearance looked quite bedraggled after his day of rushing around.

Bashfully, he said, "Hi."

"Hi, yourself." Charity opened the door to let him come through.

Xavier gasped at how beautiful the entrance was, and also at what would have been a store at one time. Slowly, he walked into the large room and looked at the seating arrangement. Glancing at the walls, there was nothing but paint to be seen around the room. The drapes across the front blended well with the choice of color. He finally turned and looked at Charity.

"Wow. This place is gorgeous."

"Thank you." Charity waved a hand toward a chair. "Sit wherever you would feel most comfortable."

"Thanks." He took a seat on one of the wing back chairs that faced a matching one, with only the coffee table between them. "I can't believe there aren't any of your art pieces in here."

"Whatever is left from the shop is at the gallery." She glanced around. "They wouldn't go with the décor anyway." Pausing, she asked, "Can I get you something to drink?"

"No. I'm good, thanks." Xavier twisted his hands together. He was a nervous wreck. "Uh, how have you been? Or maybe I should ask, where have you been?"

Charity's nerves were taut, waiting for the other shoe to drop. But she knew she could make small talk too. "I've been traveling quite a bit. Right now, I'm here for the time being. I don't know if you remember Mr. Piedmont from the gallery, but I hired him to sell my whole collection."

"I remember him well. That is some undertaking. The shop was jam-packed with your pieces."

Charity shrugged. "You know Mr. Piedmont. He likes a challenge." She paused and sighed. It was now or never. There might not be a better chance to say what was on her mind. She had waited years for this moment. A call to Georgia earlier helped her solidify her resolve to clear the air. "Look. I want to apologize to you for ignoring you those last couple of years we were together. Georgia warned me I was too full of myself, and I didn't listen to your warning that you would leave if I didn't begin to put an effort into our relationship." She shook her head and looked anywhere but at Xavier. "After I woke up one day and realized I couldn't stand another gallery event, snoopy reporters, and that you were really gone, I left town. I ran to the ends of the earth, but it didn't keep me from feeling lonely and dead inside. I blamed you for leaving me all alone, and for a few years it was easier to blame you than myself. Not only that, but I also lost all motivation to create another art piece. So, the last five years have technically been a big waste of time." She waved her hand at Xavier, keeping him from interrupting. "Oh, I enjoyed my travels, and I saw places I'd only dreamed about. But the loneliness and feeling of despair was never too far away. Georgia was my only contact in town, and she kept me sane. Well, that and a nice therapist I finally went to see, along with the drugs she prescribed." She chuckled and then looked back at Xavier. "Anyway, I wanted to apologize for my past behavior and hoped you would forgive me. It was all my fault for ignoring you and bathing in all the attention thrown my way." She blew out a long breath and tried to relax.

Xavier was shocked and sat there slack-jawed for a moment. Charity was a long way from the person he'd left behind, and it threw him for a loop. Maybe they had both matured in the last ten years. He wasn't sure how to answer her. He started and stopped a couple of times before he was able to string his sentences together. "No apology necessary, Charity. I asked to come over here today to apologize for not being more understanding of your situation. You know, after I left, I spent a few years being a workaholic, and was laser-focused on my company. I've had a lot of success, and at first I was like a proud peacock, preening at my accolades and limelight. Believe me, I thought of you many times over the early years and kicked myself senseless at the times when my ego made me a little big for my britches. Fame is quite addictive, and I found myself in some of the same predicaments you dealt with over the years. I told myself over and over that I was in the same boat you were in for so long."

It was time for Charity to be shocked at Xavier's apology. "Yes. Very addictive. I'm glad my life is more sedate now. I told Mr. Piedmont that there wouldn't be any more pieces once he sold my last one and I wouldn't do any commission work, either. I'm tired of the lifestyle that I lived, and am looking at being more introverted and away from the public eye."

"Hmm. Well, I hope you are settled into this place. I am amazed at how it looks. If I may ask, who did you hire?"

Charity blushed, pushed some hair behind her ear and replied, "I did this by myself. I also redid the old shop in a similar fashion. I had nothing but time on my hands, and, after a few false starts, I think I ended up having done a great job."

"I don't know why I'm surprised. You always had great taste." He looked around again. "This is the same color as the outside, right?"

"Yes."

They were both quiet for a few moments before Xavier finally got around to talking about him buying all the property around her. "I'm sure you've heard by now that I bought up everything around you."

"I've heard." Charity knew the time had come, and she was ready for the fight, bracing herself for what was ahead.

Offering a small smile, he continued. "I was going to tear everything down. Flatten it and tear up all the concrete, including the streets, and start over with completely new infrastructure."

"Was?"

He rubbed the back of his neck. "Yeah. Well, the conversations we were having with the city were about either a new business district or residential. The residential won because of all the money they spent refurbishing the downtown, which pulled all the business out of this area. And the traffic on the highway is atrocious, so adding an additional commercial site that might have delivery trucks could make a lot of people mad as they ramped on and off right out here."

"Like they used to."

"Right. Anyway, Buck, my right-hand man, spent a lot of time buying up all this property. Sometimes the sales went through quickly, others tried to hike up the price. Thankfully, we had a great realtor and he worked with the individuals to accept my offers, which were above property value anyway."

"I don't believe Buck ever tried to offer me any money. He would have had to go through Georgia, and she didn't know what was going on, either."

"That's because I told him I would handle it myself since I knew you. I figured we were on bad enough terms; you didn't need some stranger trying to barge his way in. Buck can get a little excited and pushy when he is working on projects."

"Unlike you, by chance?" She almost felt like she scored a point, by the look on his face, so she finished with, "So, what is your offer?"

"There's no offer."

"What? I'm confused. I thought that was why you were here."

"Nope. No offer. Not unless you want one. My plans have changed considerably since we started this a year and a half ago."

Charity sat back further into her cushions. She had been prepared to fight for her property, and this was a complete surprise. Shaking her head, she replied, "I don't know what to say, except no, I don't want to sell either building."

Xavier got up and wandered around the room. "When I stopped by to try and find you a few months ago, I was going to ask to buy your properties at that time. But the longer we looked at some of the buildings, the more we felt we could revitalize the area without disturbing the ambience. Take your property. You have done a fantastic job making your buildings look inviting. They are fresh and functional for living spaces. When you didn't fight the change in zoning, I wondered what was going on around here. I see you no longer have your shop sign up."

She nodded. "All these years, no one was caring for the buildings. I stopped by to check on things occasionally over time. Before I decided to move home permanently, I stood outside and looked at how worn and tired they appeared to be. That's why I did the facelift. That, and I wanted to make sure I got my money's worth from you if you insisted I sell and we ended up in court." She smiled, then got up to stand in front of him. "Two can play your silly games, you know."

He smiled back. "You haven't lost your touch, my dear Charity." He put some distance between them and slowly headed for the door. "Now that this situation has been settled, I will leave you be. I wanted you to know that your property is safe from my greedy little hands."

"I appreciate you stopping by and letting me know. I've wondered for months what was going to happen."

"The whole project changed in scope over the last several weeks, so I'm glad I couldn't find you the first time I stopped by. Then I was out of town for a long time. Now that we are getting started, I'll be around your neighborhood a lot. But I needed to talk to you first before the guys began tearing everything up. Anyway, it was good to see you again. And I'm glad you are doing so well. You're more gorgeous than ever too. I also wanted to confess I went to your opening at the gallery, but I didn't think you needed the press to gossip about us, so I stayed away from you. It wasn't the time nor the place to have this conversation." He bent forward and gave her a quick kiss on the cheek and was gone before Charity realized what happened.

Xavier sped back to the apartment to meet up with Buck for supper, but all he could think of was the ravishing beauty he left behind. He stopped himself, more than once, from grabbing Charity in a bear hug and kissing her senseless. Now he might have to take a cold shower before he did anything else. The visit went much better than he imagined and was taken totally by surprise when Charity apologized. He wasn't kidding when he told her he understood what she had gone through, being famous. The emotional roller coaster that his life was on for the first few years took a toll. He was the handsome, up-and-coming real estate magnate who was always in the newspaper and magazines. That was why Buck and Rainy were his most trusted employees and friends now. He learned the hard way who his real friends were. Pulling into his parking spot, he took a deep breath before heading inside. It was time to have a long conversation about Buck's day, not his. And he was thankful for that.

The men enjoyed a quiet meal, thankful that they didn't have to entertain anyone. By the time they finished, Xavier decided to talk in their suite instead of the restaurant. There was no sense discussing business where anyone could hear them, when they had a perfectly comfortable place to retire to. Kicked back and relaxing, the men continued to chat about world events and baseball before Xavier decided to get down to business.

"Okay. I told Charity we weren't going to make an offer, and she was glad about that. So now that is out of the way, let's hear what happened with the mayor today."

"All the groundwork is done, the paperwork is filed, and even though the teardown of those awful commercial buildings is already in progress, we can begin to work at full speed. Now all I need to do is find some local contractors to work on the buildings we are saving."

"Go on ahead and get some bids, but I do have an idea I'd like to have you kick around."

"What's that?"

"Have you noticed that Charity's properties have had a facelift?"

"Oh, yeah. I've been so busy I forgot about it. They look nice, but I haven't really taken a good look. Why?"

Xavier looked out the window at the fading light. "The colors are great, and I'm not sure that they don't change with the light. Since there are viable buildings on that same block, what would you think about continuing with soft muted colors like she used? Not the same ones, of course, but colors that would complement the whole block."

"You mean, like add a red, blue, green, or something like that?"

Xavier shook his head. "Not exactly. I think you need to take a good look at the colors she chose. I wouldn't want anything bright next to them. Like I said, muted colors. So even if you use a blue, it would be really pale."

"Got it. I'll have to look at her property again to refresh my memory."

"And she has done the inside with the same colors. Maybe you could ask to look inside so you know what I mean."

"I suppose I could. Your visit to her place must have really impressed you. You rarely care what colors we choose for the projects."

He nodded. "It was very enlightening, and I kept looking at the space. The place was very comfortable, and the colors were perfect. Honestly, maybe we should ask her to do the decorating. She could pick the colors to dress up each place. I hadn't realized how bland all our projects are inside. I suppose it's easier just to paint everything white."

Buck shrugged his shoulders. "I have to hire someone anyway. Do you want me to check into this idea further or do you want to approach her about this? Or was this just a thought flying by?"

"No, you can ask her. But see if you can get a look at both places. If the other building is a gorgeous as the one she is staying in, I think we may have hit a home run on design ideas."

"Okay. I'll stop by tomorrow and see if I can catch someone at home. Now, let's see, you need to go talk to the crew that is tearing up the two blocks down from there, and give them further instructions. Is Pete going to be available to bring his crew up from Missouri, or are we going to see if Dave is about done?"

"Dave, definitely. Pete has a long way to go yet, whereas Dave could start bringing some of the crew here. He can leave his finishing bunch in Minnesota, then Rainy can make sure Debra is on top of the decorating and installation of the appliances."

"Are you going to want Debra to come here too?"

Xavier smiled. "It depends on if you can sweet-talk Charity into taking it on. She's an artist by trade, so her taste is excellent. She won't skimp on quality, either. Deb will do the ordering of appliances and other stuff later. She's a pro in that area."

Buck yawned and rubbed his face. "Looks like I have my week cut out for me. I need to head out to Colorado before long. There are some hotspots I need to tend to."

"No problem. Let me know what you find out. I'll be in and out of here tending to business, but I'll stop and see the guys first thing tomorrow." He yawned. "Stop yawning. Now you're making me tired."

Buck chuckled as he got up to walk to his room. "See ya later."

Xavier didn't want to talk to Charity again if he could help it. He was afraid that he would want to start up his relationship again with her and knew that it was impossible, the way he lived. Flying from one state to another and staying for weeks at a time away from home was no way to try to revive a relationship that died from lack of attention in the first place. Shaking his head, Xavier headed to his room to take care of some computer work before turning in. It was three hours later before he'd addressed all of Rainy's emails, along with answering a dozen others. As soon as the lights were out, he thought about Charity once again. He punched his pillow and turned over. It was going to be a restless night.

Waking up to the smell of coffee, Xavier made his way to the kitchen. Buck was already gone but left a pot full of brew behind. With the lousy night he had, it might take the whole pot to get him going. It was almost ten before he got out to the construction site to see the work being completed. The first building was a big pile of wreckage, and they were starting to work on the other disastrous building. The foreman saw Xavier standing by the work trailer and drove over in his beat-up pickup to meet him.

"Glad you made it. I wanted to clear up some confusion before we hauled the material off. The first full truck headed to the recycler, but they refused it. Said it was too trashy and to take it to the dump. I made a couple of calls, and the only place we are allowed to haul this is over in Grayson County. They will have us dump it in a construction material site and they will sort through it all and do what they can with it. It's going to cost a fortune in fuel and manpower. That's a long drive."

"It doesn't sound like we have much choice."

"Nope. I guess the place here used to take stuff like this but ran out of room."

"Hire whoever you need to get it done. I don't want to lose time over an argument with scrapyards."

"Will do. And, by the way, the cement will be hauled

to a place outside of Churchtown like we planned."

"That's good news, then. At least something is going right. What else is going on?"

The men walked around the area and, using spray paint, marked a few of the old stores with a large X to show which ones needed torn down. They would cost more to repair than to replace, so there was no sense in letting the demo crew leave without removing all the dilapidated structures. By the time they got back to Xavier's car he was starved, and his stomach growled so loudly even the foreman heard it over the sound of the machinery. They both laughed, and he got in his car to go find a place for lunch. On his way to the highway, he saw Buck pull up at Charity's place. He silently wished him luck and continued on his way.

7

When Buck parked in front of Charity's Shoppe, he sat admiring the buildings. It was a few moments before he realized that the shop sign was removed. Looking at the buildings once more, he knew Xavier was right about the colors being very appealing. They didn't jump out at you and blended well with each other. As usual, his boss was right. He got out and walked up to the door. Xavier didn't mention where Charity was living, but he just assumed it was above the old shop. He knocked and waited, then knocked again. He was about to give up when he saw someone coming to the door. Once opened, Buck was speechless. If this was Charity, it was no wonder Xavier wanted to talk to her himself. The woman was gorgeous.

Martine was drying her hands on a towel as she opened the door. Thinking she heard something, she looked out the window and saw a strange car. Sighing, she figured it was probably someone looking for Charity, since no one knew where she lived except for the postman.

"May I help you with something?"

Buck tried to gather his thoughts together. He couldn't help but stare at Martine's black eyes peering at him behind her blond bangs. "Uh, yes. Are you Charity?"

"No. She lives next door."

As Martine began to shut the door, Buck reached out a hand. "I'm sorry. I should introduce myself. I'm Buck. I work for the construction company that bought the property around here."

"Ah." She shook his hand and felt a jolt of electricity go up her arm. She quickly let loose. "I'm Martine. So, you work for Xavier?"

"Yes. He wanted me to take a look inside and out of her properties because he was so impressed with her selection of colors and decorations. He visited her yesterday but forgot to tell me which building I'd find her in. I didn't realize anyone else lived here."

"I've been here for several years now. She has done a nice job on the place. I was amazed at what she could do in such a short amount of time." Martine stood in the doorway and wasn't sure what to do next. "Xavier wanted you to look at the inside?"

"Yes. He kept going on about how nice Charity's place was and that she had done them both. Would you mind if I took a peek?"

Martine looked around outside and didn't see anyone else. "Is Xavier going to try and buy these buildings?"

"No. He has no intention of doing so. But he does want to complement the rest of the block with what she has done. That is why I want to take a look."

"You can look on this floor only. I'm not comfortable allowing you into my work or living space."

"No problem. And when I'm done, I'll stop over and see if Charity is home. I need to speak with her anyway."

Martine opened the door wider and let Buck come inside. He gasped and stopped in his tracks to look around. She grinned behind him. It truly was a beautiful space. Buck eventually walked around the whole area and commented to himself on different aspects of the large room.

***

"Xavier wasn't kidding. Charity really did a fine job bringing the colors inside. She did an amazing job."

Still grinning, Martine nodded. "I know. It's wasted space on me as I don't entertain. Actually, you are the first person to walk through here since she finished decorating."

"That's a shame. What a great place to have friends over." He turned and looked at Martine. He was jolted by her eyes once again. "What do you do?"

"I sculpt. My workshop is in the back, and I live upstairs."

"Nice." He took another look around. "I appreciate you letting me check things out. I'll go see if Charity is home. And, by the way, you will be seeing me around quite a bit. I work closely with Xavier, and right now we have a lot of different crews to get scheduled."

"Good to know. It was nice to meet you."

She walked him to the door, said goodbye, and watched him go next door. Before long, Charity was letting him inside. She shut and locked the door, then leaned against it. Buck's sandy blond hair kept falling into his eyes making him look about ten years younger than he probably was. It had been a long time since Martine had been attracted to a man, and Buck was certainly a fine specimen. Sighing, she headed back to her apartment to finish washing her dishes. She would be sure to keep an eye out for that man in the next few weeks. Giggling, she dug back into the sudsy water.

Buck no sooner knocked than Charity opened the door. She was on her patio and watched him pull up. She figured he was probably looking for her, since Martine never had company. Ever. Charity couldn't fault her, since she never invited anyone over, either.

"Hi. What can I do for you?"

"Are you Charity?"

"I am."

"Great." He stretched out his hand. "I'm Buck, Xavier's all-around go-to guy."

She shook his hand. "Come on in. What can I do for you today?"

Buck stopped and looked around. "Xavier wasn't kidding when he said you did a great job decorating. Very minimalistic, but it goes with the place. I like it."

"Thank you. Would you like a glass of water?"

"I would, thank you. Mind if I wander around?"

"No, go on ahead. Through that far door is the back room. Take your time and I'll be right back."

Charity headed upstairs and Buck took his time looking at the walls, floor, and furniture. He eventually made it to the door that led to the back when he heard Charity come back down the steps. She handed him his glass of water and had one of her own.

"Go on ahead and open the door. This is pretty much empty except for my small workspace."

He stepped through and was amazed at the space available. "Are you going to do anything with this? I mean, like adding living space? I see you park your car inside."

"I hadn't planned on changing a thing. I noticed you were next door for a few minutes. Did you look at Martine's place?"

"She only allowed me in the main floor living space."

"Her back room is where she does her sculpting. We artists are pretty territorial."

"In some of the other stores, there are shelves and sometimes a big office. In a few the space is a garage. I haven't seen any made into living spaces. But this gives us so many possibilities to make more living space for people with families."

Charity led Buck back to the front and motioned for him to sit down. "Why did you stop by, exactly? I know Xavier liked my design, but what do you need?"

Buck chuckled. "I guess I didn't really say, did I?" She shook her head. "Xavier and I had a long discussion about this whole area. I know he told you we weren't interested in buying your property, but what he came up with last night might take you by surprise."

She cocked her head and looked at him with reservation. "Go on. Don't keep me in suspense."

Smiling, he waved his hand around at the space. "Your property is tastefully done, inside and out. What he would like to do is choose colors that would blend into the area. Not matching yours at all, but have the muted tones to attract people to the neighborhood. We might use a pale blue or gray, something that would separate each building by color, but not blast your eyes where you would need sunglasses to look at the house. Do I make sense?"

She shrugged her shoulders and took a drink. "Sure. That makes sense. And I would appreciate it too. I hate garish colors. Across the block and south is a loud pink store. If I remember right, they sold beach items, so maybe it was coral in color. But, nevertheless, it was bright. Not so much these days, of course."

"I know the one you are talking about. I believe we are tearing that one down. And a few more along with it. They would cost more to repair than rebuild. I'll make one more walk-through to make sure which ones we are keeping." He waved his hand around. "Do you remember how old these buildings are?"

"Now you are taxing my brain. Let's see. I believe most of them were built right after the turn of the twentieth century. If I remember accurately, both of mine were built in the 1920s. But some of those, like that pink one, were built a decade or more before mine."

"And you have updated your electricity and plumbing, I assume."

"All of that was done right after I bought them, and I have updated a few things since then too. I try to keep things repaired, but when I wasn't living here, no one really noticed the damage to the outside. Now that everything is up to snuff, I expect the place to look nice for years. I used some expensive siding so there will never have to be a paint job completed."

"Another thing I'd like to know is the name of the company you used to do your siding. I'd like to contact them for our other buildings."

"Sure. I can get you a business card. I won't need them again." She left to retrieve the information. Buck sat back and drank his water while waiting. "Here you are."

"Thanks." He glanced at the card then placed it in his shirt pocket.

"You mentioned tearing down a few stores. What exactly do you plan to do with the ones you keep?"

"We will make living spaces in them all. And if there are good back rooms, we can make a garage and more living spaces. There are a couple that have cellars, but we will be filling those in." She nodded, and he paused for a moment. "I would love to hire you to do all the design work, inside and out."

"What?" She sat upright, eyes wide and her mouth dropped open, and almost spilled her water.

Chuckling, Buck couldn't help but be amused by Charity's obvious shock. "Xavier said it was the artistic talent that made a difference in the way the place looks inside. He's right, of course. Once we get each old store repaired and made into a home, we want you to come in and do all the color choices. We have an employee who buys all the appliances and does the final walk-through, but the company always hires a decorator. Xavier thought it should be you this time. After all, you have totally impressed us with both of your homes. What do you say?"

She was still in shock and couldn't say anything for a moment. "I'll have to think about it. I'm not a decorator, nor have I been trained to be one."

"I've seen well-trained decorators do awful work over the years. All you have to do is repeat your effort from here to the other places. Piece of cake."

"And you will pay me for my time?"

"Absolutely. If you are interested, I'll have Rainy, our office manager, send you our usual contract with the details. I'll let her know how many homes you will help us with and she will prepare it from there."

"Do you have a card, so I can call you with my decision?"

"Sure." Buck pulled a card from his wallet and handed it over. "I hope you will seriously consider this job. We know it is out of your usual, but we are both very impressed with what you have done with the place."

She tapped the corner of the card to her chin in thought before lowering it and standing up. She went over to a hidden stand and pulled out one of her Charity's Shoppe business cards. The phone number and email address were still accurate, so she hadn't thrown them out. When she handed it over, Buck stood up and walked to the door, taking his cue that it was time to leave.

"I will give you a call when I decide one way or the other. When do you need to know?"

"A couple of weeks or so. If you aren't interested I'll have to hunt down someone else to do the job."

She blew out a breath. "Okay. Thank you for the offer,

I think." She chuckled, out of nervousness. "It was nice to meet you, Buck."

He turned back before he got too far from the door. "Say, the lady next door. Is she single?"

Charity's eyebrows shot up. This man was full of surprises today. "Why, yes, she is."

Buck grinned. "Thank you for the hospitality. I hope to hear a yes from you in the coming days."

As he drove off, Charity looked over at Martine's place and smiled. With the interesting turn of events of the day, she went back to her workshop and looked at the stained glass project she had been working on. Having practiced on some smaller broken pieces, she began to create for real. This piece was going to be for her apartment. The high windows were perfect to place colorful art inside to reflect the sunshine. It should glow like a prism when completed. That was her hope. If this one worked right, she would do another one or two for her downstairs area. As she began to work on the piece, Charity thought back to Buck's offer to work for them. She had never given much thought to decorating but had always enjoyed the aspect. Outside of Martine and the delivery men, she hadn't invited anyone over to see her place after the renovation. Not even Georgia and Gary.

She dropped her tools and shut the light off. It was time to quit wallowing in pity and do something. Picking up her phone, she soon set a date and time for her friends to stop by and visit. She would invite Martine too. Grinning and feeling sneaky, she would invite Buck to stop by for her answer, whatever that would be. She rubbed her hands together in glee. Martine deserved a little attention from a good-looking man. Laughing, she went upstairs to prepare a menu.

With time moving closer to her get-together, Charity called Maurice to come and be her dinner partner. She also asked if he would make a cheesecake too. Teasing her that she only wanted him for his cheesecake, Maurice agreed to attend and bring dessert. When he asked her what she was fixing for the main meal, he suggested he meet her at the grocery store to pick out the best items. They set a time and place, and Charity brought her shopping list with her.

After a quick hug, Maurice took the shopping list from Charity's hand. "Let me see your list." He perused it and shook his head. "This won't do at all. My, my. You are a bit rusty."

"Hey!" She snatched the list back. "Yes, I'm rusty, but it's my dinner. Just because I'm not a master chef like you, you shouldn't look down your nose at me."

He leaned over and whispered, "You know you can't cook." He raised his eyebrows, then wiggled them at her.

Charity couldn't help but laugh and handed him back the list. "You win. Help a poor girl out."

Maurice looked delighted, and led Charity around the store picking out items to make a supper that would meet with his approval. Knowing that she didn't have the high-end appliances, he was careful to choose food that would cook easily in her small kitchen. By the time they were done shopping, he offered to come early and help her with the meal too. After all, he was her partner for the evening. She didn't argue one bit. If Maurice wanted to make sure the meal was up to his standards, who was she to argue? Besides, he was bringing cheesecake.

When Charity called Buck to invite him over for supper, she teased him with the fact Martine had agreed to come too. He was all in after that, and didn't even ask what her answer was to the job offer. Charity felt like things were coming right along. Now she was standing there, looking at the space on the main level, trying to figure out how to fit in a large table and buffet. The old office was torn out before she remodeled, and the area was ripe for a dining table. Measuring the space carefully, she then went furniture shopping. After spending more than two hours checking out every table and chair combination, she finally chose the perfect set. And it even had a matching buffet. They promised delivery and set-up the following day, and Charity knew her special evening would be a big hit.

Once the delivery men left, Charity stood back and looked at the bare walls. She knew just the thing to spruce up the area. She pulled out a few pieces of art she had stored away, then picked the ones that would go well in the space. Satisfied with her selections, the walls were soon alive with paintings. The next few days were spent cleaning and setting up her new dining space. The buffet held the good dishes and silverware. Of course, she had to get them all unpacked and washed first. Gradually, the table was set, along with candles on top of a runner in the center. The table could seat twelve but, since she was only having half that many, she took out two leaves. It was perfect, and she couldn't wait for Maurice to give his stamp of approval. She loved the man dearly, but he was certainly persnickety. She laughed at the thought and began to clean her apartment. Especially the stove and refrigerator. The last thing she needed was him scolding her about the cooking conditions. Laughing once again, Charity realized that she hadn't been this happy in a long time. A very long time.

The evening of the party arrived, and Maurice had been there for several hours, prepping the meal. Charity stood close by and helped him as he barked instructions. She was a nervous wreck by the time the first guests arrived. Maurice kicked her out of the kitchen and sent her downstairs to entertain. He knew where everything was by now, and just needed to finish up the last important details.

Charity let Gary and Georgia in and showed them around. There was already a drink tray on the coffee table, and other drinks were set on the buffet awaiting supper. Before Georgia could say anything about Maurice, Martine showed up. Charity excused herself to help Maurice bring the food down the steps safely and set it on the buffet. Buck hadn't arrived yet, and she hoped he would show up soon. Supper was all but ready. She didn't need to worry, as Buck knocked on the door.

"So glad you made it. Supper is ready."

"Traffic was awful, and I didn't consider how much time it would take to get here."

"Come in, come in. These are my good friends Georgia and Gary. You've met Martine."

Buck shook hands with the couple and then looked at Martine. "I'm so glad to see you again." He reached out and took her hand. Not to shake, but to hold for a moment. "I'm glad Charity asked me over. I always appreciate a good homemade meal. I get so few of them."

Martine was speechless as soon as she saw Buck arrive. She was finally able to put some words together. "I'm glad you could join us." She slowly removed her hand from his and turned toward Charity with a questioning look.

Charity ignored Martine and turned to introduce Maurice next. He had just finished placing the last dish on the buffet before turning and said, "Dinner is served."

"Maurice, this is Buck. And I want everyone to know that this delicious meal is because of Maurice. All I did was provide the space and play errand girl." Everyone chuckled. "Let's have a seat, and I will begin to pass the dishes. Maurice, you sit down now. I'll handle the hard part."

He scoffed but did as he was told. Gary and Georgia sat on one side and Buck was next to Martine on the other. Maurice sat in the guest-of-honor seat at the head of the table, and Charity would face him once she sat down. The dishes were served one by one, and the table was soon filled with lively conversation. Martine was quiet at first, unsure of what Charity was up to by inviting Buck to supper. She couldn't wait to approach her later.

When supper was finished, Charity had everyone move to the living area for dessert, coffee, and conversation. Buck maneuvered his way to wherever Martine was and managed to sit close by. Maurice and Charity cleared off the table and brought the dessert. They set it out on the large coffee table, and everyone served themselves to whichever flavor of cheesecake they wanted.

Charity looked around as her friends were finishing their desserts. "I wanted to mention a couple of things. Buck came by the other day and looked at both of my properties. Then he asked me if I would oversee the choosing of colors for the rest of the old stores as they refurbished them, inside and out." Everyone oohed and awed, thinking it was a good idea. She continued. "Anyway, I told him I would get back to him after I made an informed decision. I invited him tonight and told him I would give him an answer if he showed up. Nothing like bribing a businessman." Her friends laughed and she joined in, then turned to him. "Buck, I accept your offer, contingent on what the contract says."

"Great. I was hoping you were going to say yes. I have a contract for you in my email, and I can forward that to you. Or I can print it out and drop it by."

"I look forward hearing from you. Just email it to me." They shook hands as a formality.

The evening was a success, and soon everyone was

headed for home. Charity refused to allow Maurice to clean up and sent him on his way. Of course, he left the cheesecake with her. Gary ate as much as he could while he had the chance, sneaking in his last piece on his way out the door.

Being the gentleman that he was, Buck walked Martine to her door. "I've really enjoyed the evening, but I would like to get to know you better. Could I take you out to supper one of these nights?"

"I'd like that." She was thrilled with the thought and decided to thank Charity later, instead of berating her.

"Great. Would you put your number in my phone?" He handed it over, and she typed it in quickly. Buck called the number and could hear it ringing on his end, but he couldn't hear her phone. "Do you have your phone shut off?" Then he heard it go to voicemail, so he hung up.

"No. I left it home. It's in the apartment."

"Oh." He chuckled. "I never go anywhere without mine. Well, now you have my number."

She smiled. "Goodnight, Buck. I very much enjoyed the evening."

He smiled back, and then whistled as he walked to his car. Martine went inside and found her phone. She typed in his name to attach to the number and put the phone back down. Martine couldn't help but grin, and even though she hadn't talked to Charity yet, she must have known Buck was interested in her. For that she was glad.

When Buck walked into his apartment, Xavier was stretched out on the couch watching TV with a bowl of popcorn resting on his stomach. "Hey, you look relaxed for a change."

Xavier muted the movie and sat up, almost knocking his bowl over. He grabbed it just in time. "I just couldn't answer another email. Where have you been?"

Grinning, Buck threw his keys on the side table and kicked off his shoes. Flopping into a recliner, he put his feet up, then reached over and grabbed the bowl of popcorn from his boss. Before stuffing his mouth full, he replied, "With Martine."

Xavier let Buck have the popcorn. Confused, he asked, "Martine?"

"Yeah. Martine. We had supper at Charity's."

"Hold the boat. You better start over. You two had supper at Charity's. Why?"

"Because she invited us to supper." He stuffed his mouth full and handed the bowl back.

"Okay. I am officially lost here. You better start from the beginning as to how that happened."

Buck got up to get some water and hollered behind him. "Have you ever noticed Martine's eyes?"

Xavier answered Buck's retreating back. "Yes. They are weird, aren't they?"

As he returned, Buck was grinning. "They are awesomely weird." He sat back in his chair and got comfortable.

Xavier was getting irritated because he wasn't getting straight answers. "Last I knew, you looked at the properties and offered Charity a contract. You haven't mentioned anything about being invited for a meal or

Martine or whatever since then."

"I haven't seen much out of you lately, that's why. I got a call from Charity asking me to come to supper. She said she would tell me yes or no this evening. I figured she wouldn't be saying no and inviting me to supper at the same time. Besides, she told me that Martine would be there, so I certainly wasn't going to say no. I would have changed my whole schedule to attend."

"So what did she say?"

"Martine?"

Xavier groaned. "Of course not. Charity. Did she take the job?"

"Oh. Sure she did, but it's contingent on how the contract reads."

"Did you hand it to her?"

"No. I have her email address, though, so I will send it over tomorrow. Rainy just got the contract to me in the last couple of days. I walked Martine home and got her phone number too. I'll be calling her soon."

"Buck, I've never seen you so smitten over a girl before."

He looked puzzled and pondered that statement for a moment. "I don't think I've ever been this smitten before, either." He rubbed his hands together in excitement. "I can't wait to see her again."

Xavier shook his head. "I hope you can handle her. I've seen her temper, you know."

"You irritated and interrupted her. I don't blame her a bit. You drive me up the wall sometimes too."

He shook his head, turned off the TV, and got up. "I'm headed for bed. I have to fly out first thing in the morning to Missouri."

"I'll keep the home fires burning, boss."

"That's what I'm afraid of." Buck cackled as Xavier headed to his bedroom, sat back, and munched on the rest of the popcorn.

8

Several weeks later, with the summer sun burning everything to a crisp, Xavier arrived at Charity's for a visit. He hadn't seen her since the day they apologized to each other, and he wasn't sure how much longer he could stay away. She was on his mind frequently, when he wasn't distracted by work. He had been back to keep an eye on the project but hadn't bothered Charity. Buck kept him informed of everything she was doing, but he planned to use that as an excuse to see her. Pulling up out front, he noticed right away the changes she'd made in his absence. Flower boxes were on the balcony, along with huge flowerpots out front. They were a welcoming sight, and the flowers were chosen to highlight the colors of the properties. Shaking his head at her attention to detail, he walked to the door. The sun beat down on him as he stood there waiting for her to open the door. At least, he hoped she was home. Like an idiot, he hadn't called first.

The door flew open. "Xavier. This is a surprise. Get in here out of the heat."

"I'm glad you were home. It would be nice to get a little rain shower to drop the temperature."

She shut the door behind him. "What can I do for you?"

When she smiled at him, his heart tripped, and he stuttered before answering properly. "I . . . I just stopped . . . stopped by to see how you were doing with the decorating choices."

He gulped and tried to recover. He pulled his hankie out of a pocket and wiped the sweat that beaded up on his forehead.

She frowned slightly. "How about I get you a water? You look like you could use it." Xavier nodded, and she quickly retrieved a bottle of water from her new under-the-counter refrigerator she kept by the buffet. Handing the water to him, she said, "Buck and I keep in touch. Isn't he keeping you up to date with things?"

"Yes, he is. But I like to see for myself sometimes."

"Sure. Come over here and I'll show you my process in choosing colors."

Charity led him to her dining room table. All the leaves were in, the chairs were pushed off to the side, and there was a large sheet over the table for protection. On top were a multitude of siding material and paint chips to choose from.

"As you can see, I have samples of siding in all the colors available. I automatically refused the loud colors and kept the muted ones, as you wanted. Then I have all these paint chips that I'm using to pick the trim colors with. Those will follow inside, of course. Then, as I settle on color choices, they are set to the side, and I work on another set. You wouldn't think it was difficult, but if you want everything to blend, then I not only have to match the colors but also ensure that the house sitting next to it doesn't clash."

"Sounds like a lot more work than I would have gone through."

She chuckled. "Well, think of it like this: my green

shouldn't be next to orange. Okay, that's a little extreme, but that should make sense for you. I have these two ready to order when Buck says it's time. These will go next door to me. I'm working on the last one on the block right now. He says they started next to me because my property was already done, and it would be easier to sell homes on a block that was already occupied."

"He's right. The first one to sell is always hard. Once someone is in place, then other people want to get the property before their friends. Or their enemies, sometimes."

"Jealousy rears its ugly head once again."

"Yes. I guess you're right. I believe they will work across the street next. Have you given any thought to what would be across from you?"

"There are enough colors to choose from, but just. When we get to the next block, do you want the same colors used, or are we going to be a bit brighter and bolder?"

"Hmm. I'll give that some thought and get back to you. It will be forever before we need to make that decision, though. We will be on your block for quite some time." He looked around and noticed some flickering colors. "Where are those colors coming from?"

Charity looked up from the samples to see where Xavier was pointing to the wall behind them. "Oh. That's from my stained glass. Look up at the windows."

He looked up and saw two windows with stained glass panes covering them. "Those are new. Did you make them?"

"I did."

"I love them." He shook his head. "A woman of many talents."

"I have one in my bedroom, living room, and kitchen. I started with one, then went crazy. I love the effect as the sun plays across the rooms at different times of the day." She sighed. "I threw away the first couple of attempts. They were atrocious. But YouTube is my friend, and I learned a lot of tips from watching different people."

"Are you planning on selling pieces?"

Charity shook her head vehemently. "Absolutely not. These are for my personal enjoyment only."

"Have you done any pieces like you used to for selling to the public?"

"Nope. And I don't plan to anytime soon, either. I feel like that part of my life is done."

"Really? You are so talented; I can't imagine never seeing a new piece from you again."

She shrugged. "Mr. Piedmont is quite disgusted with me too." She chuckled. "He still has several pieces of mine to sell, so he'll get over it."

Xavier reached over and touched Charity's cheek with a finger, then rubbed it gently. "I've have missed you so much these last few years. I'm glad you are happy." He pulled his hand away.

Charity had leaned into his touch and was sorry when it was gone. "Honestly, I've missed you too. Those years I was bouncing around, I wasn't good company for anyone, including myself. I had to come to several decisions, and when I came home, it felt right. Instead of grieving over losing my will to create, I've accepted that I am done with that part of my life. Forging ahead with the remodels made me appreciate being home again. Now that Buck—or, I should say, your company—has hired me to choose the color schemes, I feel more alive than I have in a long time. This gives me the artistic outlet I needed, but I can also remain out of the public eye while doing the job. And, since you will be remodeling for a long time, I can play with my stained glass, or whatever I feel like doing, in between picking out colors for you."

"I'm glad you are enjoying the job." He looked around and then back at Charity. "On another note, how about we go out for lunch?" His stomach growled loudly at the thought of being fed. He wondered why his stomach always had to betray him like that.

She laughed. "Sounds like you need to eat. How about you come upstairs, and I'll fix us lunch?"

Surprised at the invitation, he heartily agreed. They walked up the steps, and for the first time Xavier was able to see the apartment. He admired the stained glass once again and commented on her décor. Charity soon had lunch on the table.

"This is nice. I wanted to take you out, but I like this better."

"Not a problem. This is what I was having for lunch, anyway, so making a second meal was no big deal." She smiled at him, then leaned toward Xavier. "But you can invite me out for supper if you want."

He almost choked on his sandwich, and Charity chuckled before taking a bite of her own. Xavier swallowed and took a drink. "Supper, huh? You're on. How about Luigi's?"

"Perfect."

"Pick you up at sixish?"

Smiling, she nodded as she chewed. When she could answer, she said, "Perfect."

Xavier felt his stomach do flips, and it had nothing to do with his meal. This beautiful woman was going to supper with him. When he left the apartment, he called Luigi's to make sure they could get a table. It was a Thursday, so his chances were pretty good. He lucked out, and they could get in at six-thirty. The timing was impeccable, and he could hardly wait to see Charity again. In the meantime, he needed to take care of some business and catch up with Buck.

His apartment was still as sparsely furnished as Xavier remembered, but it was comfortable. After all, he and Buck spent little time there. It served as their stopping point when in town, and the beds were decent. But since they would be staying around for quite some time, Xavier figured he should find a more permanent solution. This project was going to take two or three years to complete, and there was no sense in spending a ton of money on the suite. He vowed to find a better solution while in town this trip. Of course, he had been saying that for some time, but then he was on a flight somewhere else. Right now, all he wanted to do was park himself in a chair. He and Buck sat down and put their feet up. It was a much-deserved rest for them both, even though they were going to be discussing business.

"I stopped over at Charity's place before coming to the apartment. She showed me the colors she is picking out. It sounds like things are coming along okay."

"Yeah. I've never seen anyone take so long to pick out colors before." Buck chuckled. "But I've got to hand it to her, the choices she is making will make the whole block look great."

Xavier nodded. "I agree. Did you see the stained glass in the windows?"

"I did. I wish she would add a piece or two in some of the homes, but I can't convince her to make any."

"She told me the same thing. I mean, Charity told me she wasn't going to make them to sell. Maybe down the road she will change her mind."

Buck shrugged and took a long drink of his iced tea. "Man, this tastes good. The heat is killing me." Xavier agreed. "I have a question for you."

"Shoot."

"Pete won't be done in Missouri for a long time. The rest of Dave's crew will be arriving in the next few weeks. Everything in Colorado is wrapping up. The only thing left is the rehabs in Florida, and since we hired local contractors there, what are we going to do to keep Pete's crew busy?"

"I've been thinking about that. You know Pete has been training that kid, Jimmy."

"Yeah. What about him?"

"I think we should bring Pete here to help Dave and leave Jimmy to run the crew in Missouri."

"Do you actually think Pete will allow Jimmy to take over, without complaint?"

Xavier laughed. "No, but he wants to slow down and then retire. So, this is the perfect solution. He can help Dave, Jimmy can take over Missouri, and Pete's wife will be glad to be closer to home. I think they have been missing out a lot with their grandkids' activities, and she has been spending a lot more time at home than with Pete."

"He's getting soft in his old age." They both laughed, because Pete always tried to act tough and hard-nosed, but they both knew he was a marshmallow when it came to his family.

"I haven't found any new projects, and with the Churchtown construction just getting started, I think we can keep all of our crews busy for now."

"Probably so. I'm getting tired of flying all over the place. I could use a few months in one location for a change."

Xavier nodded, got up, and filled both their glasses again. That was another reason to find a more permanent living arrangement for them. Sitting back down, he asked, "So what has been going on in your life these days?"

Buck actually blushed. "Oh, not much."

He looked at Buck, curious as to what caused his embarrassment. "I think there must be a certain someone by the way you are acting."

Unable to look at his boss, he scanned the room and then down at his phone, where he was texting Martine. "You remember the girl who lives in that old studio of Charity's?"

"Sure. She yelled at me." He paused and then suddenly realized why Buck was fidgeting. "Are you seeing her?"

"Um. Yes. We hit it off and see each other while I'm in town."

"Huh." Xavier shook his head. "She has the weirdest eyes I've ever seen on a blond."

Buck grinned. "I know. They are so cool."

He shook his head. "Well, on that note, I have a date with Charity this evening, so I better take a shower."

"Whoa. With Charity? And you were giving me a hard time about Martine."

Xavier got up and ignored Buck's jeering behind him as he headed toward his bedroom. He couldn't fault Buck for his interest in Martine. And secretly, he was happy that there was someone in his life. He and Buck had lived on the road for so long, neither one of them stopped long enough to find a woman who could put up with their long absences. But now that he was back in town, he planned to see if he and Charity could find their way back. He couldn't help but root for Buck and his new relationship with Martine, either. Smiling, he stepped into the shower and washed the hot, sweaty day off. He hoped the night would bring a new beginning with Charity.

***

After her successful dinner party, Charity became more outgoing with old friends. She began attending functions instead of turning people down. Once she began to show up around town, the invitations poured in. Charity was careful which events she attended, not wishing to be there just to be seen. Picking and choosing was difficult since she hadn't been around for several years, but a quick call to Georgia would help her decide. If Georgia was going to be there, then she would attend. It was as simple as that.

Georgia was her sounding board, and, now that they could get together more often, Charity was feeling more comfortable all the time. Many times, they discussed Xavier, and Charity finally admitted that she missed him, and there were no hard feelings. When Buck asked if she would work for the company, she saw that as an opportunity to talk to Xavier to see if there were still feelings between them. That wasn't the reason she took the job, but it may have been the deciding factor. Besides, Buck was so sweet on Martine that she couldn't help but get those two together.

The day that Xavier finally showed up on her doorstep once again, she was thrilled to see him and quickly invited him inside. The heat had been unbearable, and she felt sorry for the men working on the remodeling. The spark between the two was still there, and Charity was happy to encourage Xavier. Now that they were going out to one of their favorite restaurants, she was undecided as to what to wear. Talking to him and going out on a date were two separate things. She didn't know why she was so nervous. She had known Xavier for years, and at one time they planned to get married. The time just wasn't right for them then, but she secretly hoped they might still have a future. Finally choosing a sleek, silky gray outfit, Charity was ready by the time Xavier pulled up. She picked up her clutch and met him at the door.

Xavier leaned over and pecked her on the cheek. "You look ravishing."

"Thank you."

"I see you're ready to go. We have reservations at six-thirty, so we can take our time getting there and not worry about the traffic." Xavier helped her into the car, and then ran around and got in. "The mayor told me a long time ago about the traffic problems, and I experience it every time I try to get anywhere in town. I haven't talked to him recently, but I hope he has a plan to fix the problem."

"I have no idea, but I think the council argue and fight about it more than anything. I'm glad there is an exit close. You're going to need it for all these new homes."

Xavier nodded as he weaved through traffic. "That was one reason I chose the area. Of course, we didn't know if we were going to build a strip mall or residential homes at the time. But the final decision appears to have made everyone happy."

"Including me."

Xavier smiled at her, then pulled off the busy highway into a less traveled area. "Thank you for seeing me tonight. Or. maybe I should say thank you for being seen with me." He pulled into the parking lot at Luigi's.

She reached over and touched his arm. "Thank you for inviting me. I mean that. I have missed you more than I could have imagined."

That was all and more than Xavier could have hoped for. "I've missed you too."

They leaned into each other for a brief kiss. Smiling, they were soon seated inside, happy to be spending time with each other after all the years apart. They spent the evening catching up, and both felt like the years had fallen away. Before they knew it, the evening was over, and they were standing in front of Charity's building.

"I really enjoyed the evening." Charity unlocked the door.

"I did too. I'll call you soon."

"You better." Charity smiled. "You know, it wasn't time for us to be together a few years ago. But I hope we have both grown and figured things out since then. Maybe there is a chance for us now."

Leaning in, Xavier whispered in her ear, "I can only hope." They kissed briefly, and he was soon on his way to the car.

Charity went inside and walked up to her apartment. The evening went better than she thought it would, and hoped the two of them could find their way back. But with Xavier on the road all the time, she wondered if it was only a pipe dream. Wondering if they were destined to remain separated, she shook her head and refused to think bad thoughts after the lovely evening she'd had. *One step at a time*, she told herself.

***

Calling the realtor, Xavier lined up properties to walk-through over the next few days. A storm had blown through and finally cooled things down a bit, and for that Xavier was grateful as they got in and out of the car. Some of the homes weren't kept very cool, either. As the days wore on, he had all but given up hope on finding something suitable. The realtor actually had to talk him into seeing the last property. Turns out, it was perfect. The home had a full apartment in the basement, and he and Buck could have separate living quarters. The full backyard was great for entertaining too. The owner had gone through and painted everything a bland color, so the place was ready to make over however he wanted. The first thought he had was about having Charity pick out the colors, but he didn't want to put any pressure on their rediscovered relationship.

The location of the home was in a neighborhood not far from their new development, so they could take back streets instead of crossing town in traffic. Even though he couldn't ask Charity about choosing paint, he did want to ask her questions about furniture choices.

The phone rang several times before Charity answered. "Hello?"

"Hi. I thought maybe you were gone."

"No. I was in my workshop cleaning up and didn't hear the phone. What's up?"

"You know how I've been trying to find a place, so Buck and I weren't spending all my money on a rental space?"

"Yeah. You found something?"

"I did, and I can close rather quickly on the place. But I need furniture. I thought you could tell me where the best place would be to get a good deal on a houseful of furniture."

"Good grief. I guess you will need everything. Even the appliances?"

"I'm afraid so. But it's move-in ready, so all I need to do is buy the stuff to go inside."

"Your options are between a couple of places, but if this is temporary, maybe you want to go to the secondhand store for some things."

"No. I'll be here for quite some time, so new is best. I don't need fancy, just clean and comfortable."

"Want some help?"

"I'd love some help. Buck doesn't care what I get as long as his bed is comfortable. He cringed when I asked him if he wanted to go with me."

Charity's laugh made Xavier smile. "Tell me when, and I'll be ready."

"Are you free next week sometime?"

"Just let me know the day. I'll do a little research on the appliances beforehand. The biggest question I have is the sizes you need."

"I have no idea." He sighed. "When I get the keys, we can go over and measure first. We will plan on taking a whole day to shop. This doesn't sound like an easy job."

"Not easy, at all. In the meantime, let's do something

this weekend if you are in town."

"I need to fly out tomorrow, but will be back by Saturday."

"Call me when you get in. I'll come pick you up."

"Deal."

It was more like two weeks before Xavier and Charity went shopping. The first thing to do was to stop by the new place and write down some measurements. Charity looked the place over and made several notes, which Xavier couldn't decipher, nor did he really care. He was spending time with her, and that was all that mattered.

"Are you sure you don't want to paint first?"

"Naw. I hear a colorful throw pillow and a splashy painting is all I need. Right?" He grinned at Charity while she contemplated throwing her notebook at him.

"Okay, smart guy. Let's go."

After an exhausting day of shopping, Charity had her list completed. She then demanded he feed her well for the trouble. He had no qualms about that at all and took her to a nice restaurant. Settled back with a glass of wine, they were both tired from all the decision-making. Once they got a little food in their system, they were more talkative.

"I'll leave you with these notes and the business cards. I marked down which store would deliver which items, and they will be calling you for delivery dates in the next couple of days. Since you have so much at once, they will want to have all their guys available. If you need me to be there, let me know. Your schedule is more hit-and-miss than mine. All I do is hang out and look at color choices."

"I appreciate that. The whole day was overwhelming. I would have given up about two hours in."

"Don't think I didn't think about it myself. But it's done, and in a couple of weeks you guys can be settled into your new place."

"I appreciate this so much." He looked over Charity's meticulous notes and shook his head. "Nope. Couldn't have done it without you." He sat back, sighed, took another drink, and smiled.

"Honestly, I enjoyed it more than I thought I would. Once we got past the appliances, it was more fun."

"True. I'm glad we started with them first. I also wouldn't have thought about picking out the stackable washer and dryer for the basement apartment. That was a good idea."

"There is limited space, and that way you have the ability to move around in that small room. Besides, the guys unloading them will be happy not to have to get a full-size set down those stairs. The refrigerator will be bad enough."

He shook his head. "And the bed, couch, stove, and dining room set."

Charity chuckled. "The movers are used to it. But that's why you paid them an extra fee."

"I did?"

She nodded and smiled. "I wanted to make sure they were well compensated for such a big job."

"Are you sure they will get the money themselves?"

"While you were busy taking care of paying for everything, I talked to the men myself. I told them to make sure they got their extra money for handling such a big delivery. There won't be any way that the stores will not hand that over."

"I could have paid them on site."

"You could have. But I wanted the owner to know how much you appreciate their help for such a big job. These guys probably wouldn't have told their boss about a tip otherwise."

"I see your point. I hadn't thought of that, and I work with delivery men all day long every day of the week."

"Sometimes it's a thankless job, and they don't get paid exceptionally well for their hard work. Tips are always appreciated."

"I'll keep that in mind for the future."

A month later, Buck and Xavier were well entrenched in their new home. No longer had sharing space seemed like such a big deal until they no longer had to. Now, they both appreciated the privacy. Buck even gave up his old apartment in Oakville and moved everything into his new place. Now that Pete was helping Dave, and all available construction crews were working full speed, Buck stayed busy every day running the operation. Xavier would fly back and forth between Oakville and Churchtown occasionally, but he spent most of his time working from home and seeing Charity.

By the end of summer, the homes next to Charity were already sold, even though they weren't quite ready to be moved into yet. Her color choices had been a hit, and once the last-minute details were completed, she would soon have new neighbors. The homes across the street were under construction, and the noise during the day seemed never-ending. Where the old stores were that Xavier had torn down, those lots would wait until all the remodeling was finished before attempting any fresh construction. Xavier had his architect working on specs to match the current buildings, so any new construction would look the same age as the ones they remodeled. But no matter how busy Xavier was, he tried to remain in Churchtown as much as possible to be closer to Charity. But traveling to secure new locations was second nature, and off he would go once again.

9

The summer seemed to fly by. Martine was busy finishing her statue for Mr. Higgens's garden, and she took on a new commission for someone halfway across the state. She had driven a couple of hundred miles to see where the statue would go, and after being wined and dined, Martine finally agreed to committing to the project. She was frantically finishing her current statue during the day to meet her deadline, but the evenings would be spent either drawing specs for the new commission or seeing Buck. He was becoming a part of her life, and she appreciated the distraction from her work.

In a moment of weakness, she allowed Buck into her studio to see her latest piece. He was in awe and couldn't figure out how she could manufacture such a magnificent object out of a block of stone. The flowers and plants looked just like they had grown and bloomed right out of the base, and he couldn't commend her enough on the work. If she hadn't seen the look on his face, she would have thought he was just saying it just to please her. But the look of wonderment made her feel confident and proud of the work she was bringing to completion.

Mr. Higgens had been by a couple of times in the last several months and was impatient to see the piece in his garden. The last time he stopped by, they arranged a date for the crane to pick it up and deliver it. Wanting to have it installed before the cold weather set in, Mr. Higgens already had a party scheduled to honor his wife and show off the sculpture. Of course, Martine would be the center of attention at the party, along with the sculpture, and she wasn't looking forward to all the fuss. Buck agreed to come with her, and she was grateful she'd have him close by. Martine also invited Charity and Xavier. The more friends she had around her, the more comfortable she would feel.

Soon, the crane arrived to pick up the statue. The monstrous piece weighed so much that a special company was brought in to pick up and set the statue in place. Martine wrapped the piece to keep all the small details safe. She even had Buck help hold the padding tight as she wrapped and wrapped. Buck teased her that the sculpture would bounce if dropped. She was so worried about that happening, she scolded him to not even joke about it. He gave her a big hug and tried to reassure her. Buck couldn't be there when the crane arrived, and Martine was glad she could fret and worry without anyone telling her not to.

She followed the crane to the Higgens's residence and made sure her piece was facing the correct way and positioned directly in the center of the cement pad. Mr. Higgens chuckled as the crane operator wanted to unhook and leave but couldn't until Martine was satisfied it was where it should be. With all the wrapping, she was almost unable to tell for sure if it was centered, but she couldn't take the protection off until the crane lowered and unhooked. Once released, the driver took off as soon as he could so Martine couldn't ask him to move it anymore. She was busy unwrapping the statue and didn't notice until later that he was gone. Sighing, she knew that the statue was now in its new home, and she had to be happy with where it sat.

Mr. Higgens stayed back and watched, and as the statue became visible from all its wrappings, he had to sit on the bench. In awe at the finished project, he gasped as the final protective covering was removed.

"Oh, Martine. It is more beautiful than I ever imagined." Mr. Higgens had tears in his eyes.

She stood back and watched the sun play off the statue. The shadows of the clouds passing by almost made the piece look like it was moving. Even she was impressed, and felt a tear run down her cheek. Brushing it away, she walked over to Mr. Higgens. "I'm so glad you like it."

"Oh, my dear. Like is not the word I would use. Love is more like it. My wife would have loved this too. I can't wait for everyone to see it." He got up and hugged Martine, then stepped back but didn't let her go. Looking directly in her eyes, he said, "You are one talented lady. I thought your drawing that day was impressive, but to see it all come out of a block of stone . . ." He paused as more tears escaped. "This is more than I bargained for."

Martine, shy as always and now quite humbled, said, "Thank you, Mr. Higgens. I believe your wife helped me create this special piece. I didn't know her, but I believe this will represent her well."

Mr. Higgens hugged her again and whispered, "Thank you, Martine. Thank you." He backed up and looked at the statue again. "My children will love this too. They will be here next week."

"I'm anxious to meet them."

He took her hand and led Martine to the house. "Come in with me a moment. I have your check all made out." He led her through the patio doors and to his office. He had her sit across from him at his desk. He riffled through a drawer, then pulled out the final check. Before handing it to her, he tapped it on the desk. "Just a moment, my dear. I'll be right back." Mr. Higgens jumped up and left the room momentarily.

Martine sat looking around the room, and appreciated how the fine lines accented the angle of the desk and bookshelves. Without being told, she would know that this was a man's domain with all the leather and heavy woods, plus rustic paintings on the walls. The heavy drapes could be drawn against the hot sun, but one bank of windows looked out onto the gardens, the statue in the background. She smiled, thinking that the scene was probably his wife's touch. Mr. Higgens flew back into his office before Martine had a chance to make any other observations about the room.

Mr. Higgens sighed as he sat down. "Now." He handed over the check but didn't release it right away. Martine didn't know what to do. Smiling, Mr. Higgens let it go. "I couldn't help but tease you a bit. You looked so serious." Martine chuckled and took the check, but didn't look at it. "Once I took a good look at your lovely artwork in my wife's garden, I knew I hadn't paid you near enough."

"Oh, no, Mr. Higgens. I billed you fairly for the work. This check is sufficient."

Smiling, Mr. Higgens handed over an envelope. "I want you to have this as a bonus. Not only did you meet my expectations, but you also exceeded them."

Without looking inside, she knew there was a significant amount of cash inside, due to the thickness of the envelope. "But Mr. Higgens . . ."

"Tut, tut, Martine. You never return a gift." He smiled broadly and folded his hands in front of him. "You are a lovely girl, and your piece is much more than I expected. I can't wait to show it off. I've decided to have my staff cover it before the party, and then you and I will undrape it after the anticipation builds." He rubbed his hands together. "I'm getting excited just thinking about it."

Martine couldn't help but laugh. "All right, Mr. Higgens. I'll take the envelope and your check. And next week, when we unveil, I hope you can feel your wife standing beside you."

"I'm sure she is sitting on the bench right now enjoying it, and after I walk you out, I'm going to join her."

"Lovely." Martine got up. "In fact, Mr. Higgens, you head on out to the gardens. I will see myself to my car." He hugged her one more time, and they each went their own way from the patio.

When Martine got to her car, she looked back and could see Mr. Higgens walking to the center of the garden to sit on the bench. Smiling, she headed for home. It wasn't until she threw her purse on the table that the envelope slid out and reminded her she hadn't looked inside. She gasped as she counted out several hundred-dollar bills. She had tears once again as she thought of Mr. Higgens's reaction to her statue. It was a work of love for her, and she had never felt such a close connection to a commission before. She truly did believe Mrs. Higgens led her in completing a beautiful work of art to represent her garden and soul.

With the heat spell finally broken, the following week was going to be pleasant weather. Martine picked out a new outfit that would work for a garden party. It was elegant yet wouldn't restrict her movements. Choosing to stick with flats for easy walking and standing, Martine reminded Charity not to wear new shoes or heels to the event. They laughed as they reminisced over Charity's gallery showing and how bad their feet hurt by the end of the evening.

Charity was going to go to the party with Martine and Buck, as Xavier was called out of town. A little perturbed at him, she shrugged it off, knowing that his job could have him leaving at a moment's notice, depending on what was happening. Sometimes he was able to send someone else, like Buck. Charity had yet to meet Rainy but heard her on the phone more than once. She seemed like a no-nonsense type of woman, and Xavier had found a gem to run the office. Feeling a hint of jealousy at their easy camaraderie, Charity admonished herself for feeling proprietary. From what she understood, Rainy had her own family to care for. Although a single mom, she had a longtime companion.

The three headed to the party, and Buck and Charity tried to lighten the moment on the drive over. They both knew Martine was very nervous, to the point of almost being too scared to get into the car. Charity didn't know what to make of it, as Martine handled the dedication at the park without a problem. Buck allowed the valet to park the car for them, then folded Martine into a big hug before heading into the backyard.

"Relax. You are going to be fine."

Charity took her turn hugging Martine. "Why are you so nervous this time?"

Martine was visibly shaking. "I'm not sure. I know Mr. Higgens loves the statue"—she waved her hand at the growing crowd—"but to be put on display in front of all these rich people scares me to death."

Charity barked out a laugh. It was so loud a few people turned to look. She smiled and waved at them, then took Martine by the shoulders. "These are the same people who show up at my gallery showings. All stuffed shirts, every one of them. The only person that matters is Mr. Higgens, and he has already approved. There is absolutely no one here who will make any snide remarks. And if they do, I will put them in their place."

Martine's mouth made a big O and sputtered out a

laugh. "Good grief, Charity." She looked behind as a car door slammed. Throwing her shoulders back, she put an arm through both Buck's and Charity's arms. "Let's do this."

Buck whispered, as they began to walk again, "That's my girl." He was completely out of his element, and was nervous enough for them both, but didn't want to let on. He wished Xavier had stayed and let him go troubleshoot, but that didn't happen. He would have to make the best of it, himself.

As the small group entered the garden, Mr. Higgens broke away from his peers and came forward, a smile on his face and his hands reaching forward. "Martine. You finally made it. I was beginning to worry." He reached over and pecked her cheek.

"Mr. Higgens, these are my good friends, Buck Jordan and Charity Hannibal."

"Mr. Jordan, welcome." They shook hands. "And Charity, my dear. It's so good to see you again. I believe my wife purchased a piece or two in the past."

"I believe she did, Mr. Higgens. Thank you for remembering me."

"Not a problem. I never forget a face. Especially if that face was connected to something my wife bought." He chuckled, and the three followed suit. "Now, come on, we have a show to put on."

He pulled Martine away from Buck and Charity and began to introduce her to several people, including his children. Charity and Buck had promised not to leave her, so they followed behind at a discreet distance. Before long, it was time to pull the covering off the statue. Mr. Higgens wanted to make sure the sunlight was just right and didn't glare into anyone's eyes. With the sun an hour from setting, it was the perfect time. He asked Martine to stand on one side and handed her a small rope, then he went to the other side. A mike was set up for him to make his big announcement, and Martine stood silently watching the crowd gather. Thankfully, Buck and Charity stayed close by on the edge in case she needed assistance.

"Thank you for coming. Many months ago, I contacted Martine Kash about making a tribute to my wife, Carol. As you know, I lost her after a long battle with cancer. During her last couple of years, she spent many hours in her beloved garden, and it helped soothe her many a day. I'm sure you've seen the new statue in the park. That was done by our fair Martine, also, and was quite impressed. So, I commissioned her to create something to capture the essence of Carol. She was a dedicated mother, wife, and, in later years, spent hours creating this beautiful garden. I only hope I can keep it looking this nice." He shook his head. "Of course, I had to hire a gardener." There were chuckles from the audience. "Martine came by a couple of times to walk through and try to get a feeling for what I wanted. We talked at length the first time, walking her through the gardens and showing her where I wanted the statue. The second time, Martine walked around by herself, sat on the benches, and sketched out different views and feelings before showing them to me. The last drawing was perfect, and we both felt that it was Carol's hand leading her to create the ideal masterpiece." Mr. Higgens choked up, along with everyone else that attended. He nodded over to Martine. "I give you, Carol's Dream."

The two pulled the rope, and the covering slid behind the statue and out of view without a hitch. Everyone gasped, including Buck and Charity. The stone was beautiful, dainty in places, strong in others, but represented the garden, just as Mr. Higgens wanted. Then someone in the audience began to clap, followed by everyone else. The applause lasted a long time, and Mr. Higgens took Martine by the hand and raised her arm up between them. Then he told her to take a bow, which she did as he lowered her arm. She thought about the end of a Broadway show, how the actresses bowed, and tried to emulate them. Smiling, she was very humbled by the applause. After a second bow, she turned and gave Mr. Higgens a hug.

She whispered, "Thank you for allowing me to create this piece for you."

"My dear, thank you. As you can see, it's perfect."

He hugged her once again, kissed her on her cheek, then turned her toward his children. They each hugged her and thanked her for her work. Their father hadn't let them see it ahead of time, so they were as surprised as everyone else. Martine made her way to Buck and tucked her arm in his. Charity smiled a few feet away and then turned to visit with someone else, knowing that Buck wouldn't leave Martine's side the rest of the night.

When the trio finally made it back to Martine's, they were all tired. The party had lasted much longer than anticipated, but they did get a meal out of it at least. Charity didn't think it was as good as Maurice's, but it was passable. The following day, Martine was splashed across the front page of the paper, as well as the gossip and art sections. Her phone began to ring off the hook, and she didn't answer a single call. Charity had warned her that people would be calling to invite her to parties and events once her name was released in the higher echelons of society. Martine let every call go to voicemail. She would sort through them later. An introvert by nature, she certainly did not desire to go gallivanting all over town. Besides, she needed to settle on a design for her next project. It wasn't going to be as intensive as what she did for Mr. Higgens, but every job she took on, Martine put everything she had into it. With her phone ringing as much as it did, Martine considered putting it on silent. She was glad she hadn't, when a special ringtone told her Buck was calling.

"Hi. I picked up the paper. Would you like me to bring it over to you? You are a hometown star now."

"Good grief. I was afraid to leave the house. Charity warned me, and my phone has been ringing nonstop most of the day."

"So is that a yes?"

She chuckled. "Yes. And bring supper with you. I'm

not going to consider leaving the house for at least a month."

It was Buck's turn to laugh. "A little exaggeration there, but I'll bring us something. Any special requests?"

"Nope. Whoops, yes. A nice bottle of wine. We can sit on the patio. The weather is perfect."

"Got it covered. I'll be by in a couple of hours. I need to go home and shower first. I helped clean out an attic today." He shivered. "Gross."

"Sounds like it. I'll see you soon."

Buck brought a full-course meal with him, and they sat on the balcony patio enjoying the evening. Martine read the articles several times and couldn't believe how much effort the paper put into making her famous. She hoped it would blow over soon.

"Have you listened to your voicemails?"

"I started to earlier today, and they were all gushy and wanted to invite me to some party or such. I quit listening. Charity was right about them all."

"Maybe there is some work in there somewhere."

Martine shook her head. "I doubt it. But I'll listen to them tomorrow. I don't know if I need to respond to each one of them or not. I'll talk to Charity about it, and maybe she can help me weed through them all."

"You're lucky to have her."

"Yes, I am. She started out as a mentor and has become a dear friend. But she still mentors me, and for that I'm grateful. She lived through being famous without anyone to help her, so I take her suggestions to heart."

Buck nodded and looked off to the horizon. "Xavier did that for me. Charity taught him a lot about being famous, and he tried not to make the same mistakes she did. I kind of got a big head when he made me his sidekick, but he took me down a notch or two on occasion. He and I have been through a lot together, and we learned that everyone is looking out for themselves." Buck sighed and turned toward Martine. "Xavier was taken advantage of more than once by someone he considered a friend. His circle of friends became smaller and smaller over a short period of time. For several years now, it's been me, Pete, Dave, and Rainy. Everyone else who works for us are well taken care of, but they are employees, not friends. So having Charity is a blessing, and I think it's a good idea for her to help screen those calls."

"Hmm. I hadn't thought about Xavier and Charity's past relationship for a long time and forgot what happened to them that caused the friction all those years ago."

"I hope they can work past that, but Xavier is gone a lot. I'm not sure their fragile relationship can take the stress. After all, it fell apart when Charity wasn't available, so I can't see how it would work with Xavier gone now."

Martine shook her head. "Then there is us. You travel a lot too. And I like to be here in my workshop. So where does that leave us?"

"Believe me, I've thought of that multiple times."

Buck fidgeted in his chair, then settled back again. "Martine, I fell head over heels for you the minute you came to the door. I was so happy to find out you weren't Charity that day." He looked away. "I'm not sure what will happen in the future, but for now, I'm here. And I will be here for about two years. But after that? I'm not sure. I gave up my apartment in Oakville, so my home office is here now." He looked back at Martine. "And if I have to quit working for Xavier to keep you in my life, I'll do that."

She was shocked at Buck's revelation and wasn't sure what to say. "Wow. You don't hold back, do you?"

He shook his head vigorously. "You can ask Xavier or Rainy. I haven't had a serious relationship since I was twenty. My feelings for you hit me hard, and I have enjoyed learning more about you every time we are together. And the one thing I have always wanted to know and was afraid to ask is where you got those black eyes from?"

Martine's emotions were all over the place. She really liked Buck, too, but wasn't sure she liked him as much as he liked her. Before she had the chance to think a response through, he threw out the question about her eyes. She jerked at the change in direction of his statement, then laughed. The more she thought about it, the funnier it was to her. Before long, she was almost rolling out of her chair. Buck wasn't sure what was so funny, but her laughter was contagious. He chuckled a little as she finally caught her breath and wiped the tears from her eyes.

"Oh, my. Here you were being so serious about us, and then you threw out the question about my eyes." She snickered again. "Usually that's the first thing a guy asks me. Sometimes they are just curious, but some people are really rude about it too. So, when you didn't ask me right away, I figured my eyes weren't a big deal."

"No. I wanted to know immediately and even asked Xavier about them. Of course, he had no idea. But I didn't want to jump you about them right off, and then I never found a good time to approach you about them again. I get a little sidetracked when I'm with you. I can't believe you agreed to go out with a guy like me."

"A guy like you? There's nothing wrong with you. I can't believe you wanted to date me. That time at Charity's you never left my side. At first, I was upset with Charity and wanted to talk to her, but she continually ignored me. But by the end of the evening, I was having a great time and enjoyed talking with you."

Buck smiled. "So now would be the appropriate time to tell me about your eyes." He wiggled his eyebrows at her to make her laugh.

"All right, all right." She smiled at Buck's silliness. My father is part native American, and I inherited his black eyes. My mother is blond, and I managed to get her hair coloring. Actually, I look a lot like my mother except for the eyes. But my father is the one I get my artistic talent from. He did a lot of wood carvings for years. He never made a living doing them, but he didn't care. Dad loved sitting around whittling, and when he had an idea for something bigger, he made it. He would give pieces away most of the time. We recently lost him, and it was just before I made any significant money sculpting. But he was my biggest champion, urging me on. Early in my career, he helped me develop my style and cheered when I sold my first piece. He always told me I would make it big. I never believed him until now."

"That explains a lot. Your dad would be so proud of you. I'm sure he's looking down and nodding his head and bragging about you to everyone."

"I'm not so sure of that. I mean about the bragging part. He was a quiet man and very humble."

"I believe you got that trait from him too." Buck leaned forward and took Martine's hands in his. "I am very serious about this relationship and am taking our being together as an important part of my life. I don't want you to think of this as a fly-by-night deal, Martine. I truly have fallen for you, and I hope you will feel the same way about me someday. But I'm not in any rush. You are a special woman, and I appreciate you more than you know." He leaned forward and gave her a loving kiss, then gradually moved back. Taking his wine glass, he finished off the rest, set the glass down, and stood up. "I need to go home and let you get some rest. It's been a trying couple of days for you. Did you get any sleep last night?".

She followed suit and stood beside him. "Not much. I kept seeing all those people surrounding me and congratulating me on my statue. I was exhausted. I guess I still am. What with this glass of wine, though, I should be able to sleep tonight."

They picked up their dishes and cleaned up the supper mess. "I'll leave the wine, and we can have it in a couple of days. I don't want it to lose its flavor."

"We certainly wouldn't want that to happen." She tucked the bottle away. "Stop by Thursday night if you can, and I'll cook supper."

"I'll plan on it but will call if something comes up."

He kissed her goodnight and let himself out. Martine went back to the patio and waved goodbye as he backed out of his parking spot and took off for home. She locked the patio door, finished her glass of wine, then started the dishwasher. Once in bed, she thought about Buck declaring how much he had invested in their relationship. Martine shook her head. She hadn't even considered it, since she figured he was only going to be here a short time. Martine enjoyed their time together immensely but had been holding her feelings back the best she could, so that when he left she wouldn't be devastated. Saying he would quit his job to stay with her shocked Martine to her core. She hadn't had a long-term commitment for years, either. Mostly because she was always locked away in her workshop. But she had been hurt before and didn't feel like the risk was worth it. *Was Buck worth the risk?* she asked herself. The only answer she could come up with was, *Yes, yes he was.*

10

When Xavier cancelled his date to Higgens's party, Charity was upset. She tried to convince herself that it wasn't important, even though she was feeling quite deflated. Charity was glad she could tag along with Martine and spend the evening close by her side to offer moral support for the girl. The more famous she became; the more Martine hid away. If it weren't for Buck, Martine might never leave her home. She was pretty much a recluse in the first place. That's why, when Buck mentioned his interest in her renter, she was all over getting the two together. So far, it seemed to be working out. If she only felt that good about restarting her relationship with Xavier.

When the two of them were together, she felt that he was somewhat hesitant to talk about their future. They had gone their separate ways several years ago, and hopefully learned a few hard lessons along the way. Charity knew she had, and was in a whole different place in her life these days. She felt almost settled for the first time in years. Xavier was still a real estate magnate and spent a lot of time flying here and there. He didn't talk about his business much, but their friendship was being repaired little by little. A quick kiss here and there, the two laughed easily. Then Xavier disappeared into his world once again. Charity kicked herself when she occasionally thought he was doing it on purpose to teach her a lesson. But then they would spend time together again and all was right with the world.

Talking it over with Georgia, Charity knew that she would have to approach Xavier about his long-term plans because he didn't seem interested in bringing them up with her. She also knew his home office was in Oakville. Where did that leave them? As the weeks flew by, insecurities seemed to grow. Were they going to be a couple again? Was he just using her as a stopover? How many girls did he have in all the cities he routinely flew into? Georgia tried to quell her thoughts, but every time Xavier cancelled his plans with her, the more she wondered if he was becoming tired of the relationship once again. It was time to put an end to her agony and find out.

Charity was the happiest working in her studio, now that her creative juices were back. She had moved on from stained glass for her apartment to trying her hand at painting. Twenty or twenty-five years ago, she was painting landscapes, and a few were now exhibited on her walls. She had forgotten how much pleasure painting gave her. It wasn't until she switched over to creating glass pieces that she became famous. No one was interested in her paintings, but her inventive art in glass became an instant hit. Charity dug through her storeroom and pulled out a few more canvases. The high blank walls were perfect for making a collage, but she would need help. A tall ladder just wouldn't do, and she didn't want to rent scaffolding again. It was time to call in some help. Taking the paintings to the living room, she lined them up along the wall and critiqued each one. Chuckling, she thought it was no wonder people didn't buy them. Her earlier works were certainly nothing to brag about. The paintings represented her coming of age, and she was finally ready to display them. Not that she had much company these days, but they would be a constant reminder of where she started. Reaching for the phone, she grumbled to herself while shaking her head.

"Mr. Piedmont, I have a favor to ask."

"Whatever it is, it's a yes."

Charity chuckled. "That was easy." She heard a muffled laugh on the other end.

"What do you need, my dear?"

"I dragged out all my old paintings and want to display them on my walls. I need your critical eye and someone to hang them. Would you be so kind as to help a girl out?"

"Paintings? Are these the ones that you thought were good enough to sell all those years ago?"

She hesitated. The man was brutally honest and had a memory like an elephant. "Yes." Sheepishly, she added, "I'm not trying to sell them, but I'd like to get them out of the storeroom and on the walls. They remind me of the young girl I once was."

"Ah. Before you became famous. I understand. Let me look at my schedule." Charity heard him turn a few pages. Mr. Piedmont always carried a small calendar book with him. "Yes, yes. I see I have a few hours available next week. I can bring Hector and Jim with me.

How many do you have?"

She did a quick count. "I have about twenty out right now, and there are a few more in a different closet. All of them are different sizes."

"Yes, well, you know I would do anything for you. I will see you Tuesday at one. Caio, darling." The phone went dead.

Charity looked at the phone in her hand. "Caio to you too." She laughed and put her phone down. Looking back at the large blank wall, she knew it was the right decision. On that note, she decided to find the rest of her paintings.

Charity spent the rest of the day cleaning frames and making them all shine. Sitting with her back against the wall, she was just finishing the last few when her phone rang. Looking at the screen, she saw it was Xavier. Sighing, she decided to answer, even though she was still aggravated with him.

"Hello?"

"Hi. Are you busy?"

Tersely, she replied, "Yes. Did you need something?"

Xavier paused. "I'm sorry to interrupt. I can call back later this evening."

Charity closed her eyes and blew out a tired breath. "That's okay. What's up?"

"I just wanted to let you know I'll be back in town by tomorrow evening and wondered if you wanted to go out to supper?"

"I don't know. Why don't you check back with me once you are back in town? I'm not sure what my schedule is like right now."

"Uh, sure." Xavier paused. "I guess I'll let you go. I'll call tomorrow, once I get to my house."

"That's fine. Talk to you tomorrow." She promptly hung up.

Opening her eyes, she thought about kicking herself for how rude she was, but she seriously wasn't in any mood to talk to Xavier right now. She still hadn't decided how to discuss their future, or even if they had one. Absently picking up where she'd left off polishing, she finished the last frames and got up. Charity had been sitting in one spot too long and groaned as she stretched and moved around. Putting her cleaning supplies away, she glanced back at the paintings before going up to her apartment. It had been a long time in coming, but she was happy to finally get them hanging once again. She refused to allow herself to think of Xavier that evening and busied herself eating a hot meal while watching a movie. Tomorrow would come soon enough.

***

Xavier had the strangest feeling that Charity was mad at him for something. He had no idea why, but her response wasn't the usual "happy to talk to you" voice. He shrugged his shoulders and went back to his meeting. They had taken a quick break because the negotiations weren't going well. This seemed to be par for the course these days. If he was going to keep his crew working, he needed to come up with some new projects. It was a good thing the current one in Churchtown was going to last a long time. Frustrated with the way the meeting was going, and now the short conversation with Charity, he was ready to go home. Not bothering to sit down once everyone returned to the room, Xavier let his frustrations be known.

"I have been here for hours discussing options, and now, if you will excuse me, I'm leaving." Every person in the room began to blame each other for Xavier's sudden decision. He whistled to get their attention and the room quieted. "You are all acting like kindergarteners." He shook his head. "Do not, and I mean do not, call me again. There is no way I will work with any of you again."

With that he stormed out of the room. He could hear the room exploding with yelling and screaming behind him, and it made him rush faster to get out of the building and to his car. Snarling at the slow traffic, he finally pulled into a practically deserted parking lot and got out of the car. He paced the lot for a few minutes to get his temper under control. He hadn't been this mad for years. Leaning against his car, he thought back to the meeting and realized he knew going in that it would be a waste of time. But he was feeling an urgency to find a new project to keep his employees busy, and was stressed to the max. Shaking his head, he noted that the restaurant right in front of him was open, so he went in to cool his heels for a few minutes.

Choosing to sit at the bar, he settled on to a stool and picked up a menu. Lunch had been a terrible concoction of items that had no taste, and what little he'd eaten had worn off hours ago. He read the menu front to back before ordering. Nursing a cold brew, Xavier thought back to the meeting and how it had all been a waste of time. People changing their minds at the last minute after the details were already under contract was not only unprofessional, but also the behavior in the room was borderline childish. What upset him more than anything was the brush-off he received from Charity. He puzzled on it as he ate his hamburger, not tasting a thing. Finishing his meal, he pulled out his phone and frowned at all the calls he'd missed. Most of them were from the people he'd walked away from that afternoon. He swiped them into the trash without listening to the voicemails, then called Rainy.

"Boss. How's it going?"

"It isn't. Do you think you can get me back to Churchtown tonight?"

"Hmm, probably. I'll see if I can change your ticket."

"Thanks. Also, have any of those people I was meeting today called the office?"

"No. Why?"

"Tell them I do not want to do business with them. I've already mentioned it, but they aren't taking it well. I have several messages on my phone."

"Got it. Anything else?"

"Do I need to be in the office anytime soon?"

"No."

"Good. I'm staying in Churchtown for a few days."

"No problem. I know how to find you. And while we were talking, I got your flight switched. You leave at eight, so get a move on."

"Thanks. I need to get to the hotel and check out. Talk to you later."

"Roger and out."

Xavier chuckled. Rainy always had a way to make him laugh, even when he was stressed past his limits. Leaving a large tip, Xavier headed for the hotel. A quick shower and a change into casual clothes, and he was soon on the way to the airport. He arrived home close to midnight and noted that Buck was still up. He could hear the muffled music playing. Dropping his suitcase on his bed, he went to the stairwell and called out Buck's name as he descended.

"Buck! You decent?"

"Yeah. Come on down," he yelled back.

Xavier popped into the living room where Buck was lounging on the couch. "I need to visit a minute."

Buck sat up and stretched. "I thought you weren't going to be back until tomorrow?"

"Change of plans. The whole thing was a dumpster fire and a waste of time."

"Shoot. Are you going to try again?"

He shook his head. "Naw. You should have seen the fighting between them. It was ridiculous. I walked out. So how was your day?" He grinned at Buck.

"Not bad. I put out a few fires of my own today, and for some reason I couldn't relax enough to go to bed yet."

"Things going good with Martine?"

"Yip."

"Good."

No one said anything, so Buck asked, "What was on your mind?"

Xavier shrugged and shook his head. "I had a strange response from Charity today. I called her to let her know I'd be back in town by tomorrow evening and wondered if she wanted to go to supper. I got a lukewarm response to my call, and then she was vague about whether she was busy or not. I'm supposed to call her tomorrow and check to see if she is available. What is up with that?"

"Like I would know?"

"Did I make her mad or something? I have no clue."

Buck stood up and stretched again. "Look. She's a woman. We have no idea what they are thinking. Even after they tell us, I'm not sure we know. But I'm ready for bed, so you are going to have to figure this one out on your own."

Xavier got up, gave Buck a fist bump, and headed toward the stairs. "See you tomorrow."

After a restless night, Xavier sat at the kitchen table and read the morning paper. He hadn't missed a thing while he was gone, so he tossed it aside. Nursing another cup of coffee, he thought about calling Charity or stopping over. Something was eating her, and he needed to get to the bottom of it. Just as he was going to pick up his phone, it rang.

"Pete. What's up?"

"When you get back to town, could you stop by the site? I need to talk to you about something."

"Sure. I got in late last night, so I can swing over there in a couple of hours."

"Great. See you soon."

He no sooner hung up when Rainy called. "Boss, we have a problem."

"Now what?"

"Those developers are saying we broke our contract and are going to sue if we don't go through with the project."

Xavier sighed. Closing his eyes, he rubbed them and then almost pulled his hair out in frustration. "This sounds like a job for Ken to handle. They are the ones who broke the contract by wanting to change everything. I refuse to deal with them again. Ken can keep them in court for years if necessary. Have him look at the original contract, then he can contact the lead person. Once they've talked, have him call me as to the plan of action. I can't deal with their nonsense. Besides, we always have the clause in our contracts for us to back out."

"Got it. I figured as much, so I already sent the contract over. I will follow up and let him know what you said."

"Thanks. By the way, I got a call from Pete this morning. Have you any idea what's on his mind?"

"Nope. But if he called and needed to talk, there must be something important to talk about."

"That's what I thought. Okay. Later."

Glad that his house was in a low-traffic area, Xavier found himself talking to Pete in no time. He had driven around the four-block area and was impressed with how busy everyone continued to be. Knowing the winter weather could slow much of the construction down, his crews pressed on. The stark landscape where the large warehouses used to be remained an eyesore, but they would remain that way for several months as they worked on rehabbing the older stores into homes.

"Hey, Pete. What's on your mind?"

Pete looked around and noticed a few guys within hearing distance. "Let's go for a walk."

"Sure." They walked toward a couple of vacant lots where old storefronts once stood.

"I'm going to retire, boss. Millie found out she has cancer, and I need to be home."

"Good grief. How long have you known?"

"For a few months. She started with radiation and will have to go through chemo now, so I need to be home with her."

"Of course you do. And you've been wanting to retire anyway, right?"

"Yeah." He scratched his scruffy beard. "I should have done it sooner, you know? You look back and wonder why you make the decisions you do. I hated to quit, even though Millie has been asking me to for a couple of years now. Then this came up. I'm glad I'm so close to home. It's made things easier for me to run back and forth, but I need to pull the plug now."

"When are you thinking?"

"Today is my last day. I've been talking to Dave about it, and he knows you don't need both of us around here. And Jimmy is finishing up in Missouri. I talk to him occasionally, and it sounds like they will be done with the construction element in a couple of months. They've had some serious rain delays, but it wasn't anything he couldn't handle. You can bring the crew here to start on the condos when he's done."

"I'll call Rainy and she will get your retirement plan and vacation all settled by the time you get to the office tomorrow. You know I couldn't have built this business without you?"

"I know." Pete laughed. "You and I made a great team. I guess that's why it's been so hard to quit. What will you do without me?"

"Honestly, I'm not sure. And right now, all my current projects are winding down except for this one. I won't be able to keep everyone employed at this rate."

Pete slapped Xavier on the shoulder, then brought him in for a hug. "You'll be just fine. It will all work out."

The hug was mutual, and a couple of tears formed, but neither one would admit it. "Don't be a stranger, and keep in touch with me about Millie. You tell her I'm thinking about her."

"I will." They headed back to the others, but just before they got back, Pete turned and stopped walking. "There is nothing I've enjoyed more than watching you grow up, boss. I mean that. You've turned into a fine man over the years. I wasn't so sure at first, but after you got through the dilemma with the backstabbers, it really changed the way you saw the world. I've been honored to work with you."

Humbled, Xavier watched as Pete joined the rest of the crew and began bossing them around. "Thanks, Pete." He knew Pete couldn't hear him, but that was okay. He turned to his car, determined to see Charity next.

But Charity wasn't home, or she wasn't answering the door. He called her phone and only got the voicemail. He left a message that he was home and hoped she would call him back. Driving slowly away, he wasn't sure where he needed to go next, but found himself back home. At odds, with nothing to do, he sat down on the couch and looked around. Sighing, he called Rainy and told him about Pete. The corporation had been covering his insurance for many years and would continue to do so for another year. Rainy would make sure of that. A bonus would also be added to his final check. Pete was someone that Xavier could always count on over the years, and he would do whatever he could to help Pete and Millie out now. Xavier settled into his recliner and closed his eyes. He was exhausted from the traveling and all the stress from the last couple of days. A nap would do him just fine. Turning his phone to silent, he closed his eyes.

11

Setting all the groceries on the counter, Charity noticed her phone blinking. Shrugging it off as a telemarketer, she emptied the bags and tidied up the kitchen. Fixing herself a cold drink, she sat down in her recliner and watched the light blink on the phone. It was driving her nuts. Sighing, she pushed the button to listen to the messages. The first one was from Martine to get back to her about more invitations. She and Martine had been going through her invites, and Charity tried to be impartial while helping her make decisions. Martine was declining many of the callers, saying she was too busy to socialize. Now that she had a client out of town, that meant long hours in her studio. Between seeing Buck and working in her back room, Martine felt no need to hobnob with socialites. There were people wanting to commission her work, but only to say that they had a piece, not because there was a heartfelt reason. Martine took her work seriously, and statues like the one in the park and Mr. Higgens's garden meant something to not only her but to the people who commissioned them. She had an appointment with an associate of Mr. Higgens, and was afraid to say no. Charity called Martine back. The rest of the messages could wait.

"What's up, girl?"

"I'm headed over to Mrs. Childress's place. Do you want to go with me for moral support?"

"No way. Even I'm scared of Mrs. Childress."

"Some friend you are."

"What was it she was wanting?"

"I figured she wanted something like Mr. Higgens's, but I'm not going to do it. That was a once-in-a-lifetime sculpture. I don't think I could ever create something that special again."

"Why not?"

"It was just the feeling I had while working on it. You know? I've told you about feeling Mrs. Higgens around me the whole time. And I haven't had that feeling since we placed the statue."

"Got it. After you listen to what Mrs. Childress wants and you decide you want to say no, you can explain that to her. Who knows? She might actually understand."

Martine mumbled something under her breath. "I've got to go. You sure you don't want to come with me?"

"No way, no how."

"Spoilsport." She sighed. "Okay. I'm outta here."

"Good luck!"

With more messages left on the machine, she clicked to listen to the rest. The next two were from telemarketers, which she deleted immediately. The last one was from Xavier asking her to call back. When she tried to call him back, it went straight to voicemail. She hung up without leaving a message, then sat back with her drink. Avoiding Xavier is what she used to do in the past and reprimanded herself for doing so again. It seemed like the past was always getting in the way of their future. She didn't know what they could do to alleviate the problem. Now that *she* was settled, *he* wasn't, and it never seemed to be a good time for them to be together.

Waking up from a long nap, Xavier felt sluggish and wasn't even sure where he was for a moment. Napping was seldom on his schedule, and this one turned into three hours. He washed his face in cold water to wake up, then headed to the kitchen to try and find something to eat. After digging around, he found an old granola bar. It would have to do until he bought groceries. Picking up his phone, he saw several text messages and a return call from Charity, without a message. Frowning, he thought he'd better take care of work first before calling Charity back.

"Rainy, what's going on? I see you sent several messages."

"First of all, are you okay? It's not like you to not get back to me immediately."

"To be honest, I was napping."

Rainy let out a burst of laughter. "Wow. Seriously?"

"Afraid so. The last couple of days were buggers. So, what do you need?"

"You need to come to the home office for a couple of days. There is some stuff we need to take care of. And I mean now."

Xavier closed his eyes and cursed under his breath. "Good thing I took a nap. I'll drive up and be there this evening. When do you need me?"

"First thing in the morning. Outside of a couple of

other things, Ken will be here about ten to go over the debacle from those idiots you walked out on."

"Great. Looking forward to it." Sarcasm dripped off his words.

"I'm sure you are. I'll see you bright and early in the morning."

It was a good thing he handled work details before he called Charity. Supper wasn't going to happen tonight. He sighed and called her back.

Charity answered on the second ring. "Hi."

"Hi. Are you okay?"

"I'm fine. How about yourself?"

Sighing again, he said, "I guess I'm all right. I just got a frantic call from Rainy. I need to go back to Oakville immediately. There is a bunch of stuff going on I need to handle. As soon as I hang up, I'll be headed out." He could hear some mumbling. "What did you say?"

"I said, okay. Whatever."

"I know I haven't been very accessible lately, and today is no exception. Duty calls and I have to go."

"I know, I know. Call me when you get back and plan to stick around for a couple of days. We need to talk."

They hung up and Xavier knew that the words "we have to talk" meant that it was the end of their relationship. He didn't have time to deal with it now. Which was too bad because that was exactly why they were in trouble. He was always gone and had to cancel too many dates with her. Before heading to Oakville, he sent a message to Buck to let him know where he was off to next. Nothing this last couple of months was going according to plan. Everywhere he flew, the deals weren't worth his trouble. Now, something was going on at the home office. On the long trip back to the office, his mind kept going back to Charity, but he couldn't come up with a logical answer to their situation, either. Everything in his life looked like it was going down the drain. Fast.

Throwing his suitcase down on the floor just inside of his Oakville apartment, Xavier groaned and leaned against his door. He was sick of traveling. The realization hit him hard. He had enjoyed running around the country making deals here and there, satisfied that he was not only securing his future, but providing jobs for many others while he was at it. The last year had proved to be depressing. Opportunities that looked good from afar turned into overblown sell jobs. Now this latest issue with the group he'd walked away from was irritating him. When you sign a contract, you stick with it. As far as he was concerned, they broke that contract the minute they tried to change the outcome. He hoped Ken would have some answers for him tomorrow. Sighing, he grabbed his suitcase and headed for the bedroom. A hot shower and something to eat would help him settle down for the evening.

The apartment was in the same building as Xavier's office. When he bought the building all those years ago, he remodeled the offices on the second floor above his storefront into his own private suite of rooms. Then he made a back access to and from his office, which was walled off from everybody else in the building. The apartment felt stuffy and closed-in after living in the house in Churchtown. He ignored the feeling and took a long shower, then dressed to run out to the deli down the street. Instead of eating there, Xavier decided to take it back home. He was too tired and upset to run into anyone he knew. He almost made it back before being stopped by an acquaintance for a few minutes. He begged off further talk, saying he had to get on a call, and didn't even care if he sounded rude.

The night dragged on, and he was almost glad when the morning sun awakened him. He grabbed a mug of coffee and went down to the office, where Rainy was anticipating his arrival. With no one else in the office, he sat down by her desk, letting out a big sigh.

"Okay. Let's get started. I can feel the bad news and need to get on with solving the mess."

"I'm sorry I had to drag you back here already, but the auditors are coming in about an hour, and they will need to discuss the books with you."

"Already?" He shook his head. "It seems like we just gave them the information the other day."

Rainy chuckled. "A month ago. And they had a cancellation so they asked if they could come. Since I had you coming back anyway, I said yes. Besides, you pay them for a reason. They've caught things in the past that our CPAs didn't."

"I know. They are helpful, and I appreciate their diligence. Will I be done in time to meet with Ken?"

"That's why they are coming so early. They didn't think it would take very long. Maybe an hour."

"That's good news, then. What's next, besides Ken?"

"Stormy is leaving town and won't be able to work for us anymore." Stormy was Rainy's sister and was hired at the same time, working part-time in the office to keep the employee data up to date.

"Crap."

"She's going to finish out the month, but I need to hire someone to take her place before Stormy leaves so she can train them. She also agreed to come back later to help train if we can't find someone before she goes."

"I suppose there are some things she can do for us from afar to get us by. I know there is a lot of paperwork involved that has to be done in the office." Sighing again, he felt the day pressing down on him more. He looked at the clock. "What else do I need to know right now?"

"Jimmy called and said that he isn't coming back from St. Louis. When he finishes the project, he is going to sign on with someone local. He found himself a sweetheart and they are going to get married."

Xavier rolled his eyes, then closed them. He thought about Charity briefly, then looked at Rainy. "What about the crew?"

"I have no idea who we will get back at this point. Jimmy says he is about six weeks out from finishing. They had a great stretch of good weather and managed to catch up and get ahead of schedule. He says the finishing crew won't need him, so he will be bailing early."

"Darn it. Pete was happy with how he turned out after all that training."

Rainy shrugged her shoulders. "That's the way it goes in this business."

"Okay. Send Buck or someone to go down and talk to the crew to find out who is committing to return. I'm not sure I'll need anyone anyway. All the projects except Churchtown are finished, and I'm not sure where I stand on this other contract."

"We can send Alan down. He is already retired, and loves it when I call for help. This will give him a chance to feel important one more time. I'll even let him take his wife on this one."

"Alan. That's a good idea. He probably should have completely retired a few years ago, but I know he likes to keep busy."

"I'll have him take care of that, then. Let's see. The auditor, Ken, Stormy, and Jimmy. I think that it's for now unless you need me to handle something."

"Nope. I'll wait for the auditors in my office. Just send them back when they arrive."

"Will do. Now. I'll get my phones switched from the answering service and get to work. It looks like I have several messages waiting."

Xavier's office was small for an executive, but he wasn't one to flaunt his success. He made a pot of coffee and refilled his mug. Rainy had a tray of pastries set aside, so he helped himself to one. Not realizing how hungry he was, he devoured the first one and picked up a second just as the auditors arrived. They made small talk and helped themselves to coffee and a pastry. Sitting at the conference table, they spread out their papers and began going over everything.

"Xavier, all in all, your books look fine, and we didn't find anything unusual or suspect."

"That's great. At least my CPAs are still doing their job."

"Correct. And with the flow of money you have coming and going, someone needs to keep a close eye on everything. And that is one of the reasons we wanted to meet with you right away. We noticed a considerable change in the funding of your business. You haven't had the expenditures like in the past, and wondered if we were given all the information we needed."

"I haven't bought any new properties since the big one in Churchtown a year or so ago. I have a contract with someone, but that deal looks like its headed south. All I have left is finishing the projects in Missouri and Florida, plus the big one we recently started in Churchtown."

"We just didn't want to miss anything. Your financials look fine, and you are still solid with a strong profit." They flipped to the right page and pointed out the final tally.

Xavier leaned back in his chair, steepled his fingers in front of him, and tapped them on his chin. "What do you think the company is worth if I sell it?"

The men's eyebrows raised, then they glanced at each other before sorting out a different page of the financials.

"I'd say this number would be about right. Maybe a little more if they trade on your name. We didn't realize you were thinking about selling."

"I didn't either until right this minute." He chuckled and leaned forward. "Don't mention it to Rainy, for heaven's sake."

"Mum's the word. I have another client in South Dakota who might be interested in buying your company."

"Really? Interesting. I need to keep some of my property for income over the years, and the ones in Florida and Churchtown will be non-negotiable. Everything else can go. Will that affect the price?"

"I doubt it. The Churchtown project is barely off the ground, right?"

"Right. And Florida is where my parents live."

"If it's all right with you, we will contact the company and see. They can call you directly if interested."

Xavier pulled out a business card and scribbled his personal cell number on the back. "If they are seriously interested, feel free to send them whatever they need to see that I own a solid business."

"Great. With that, I guess we should scoot out of here and let you get back to work."

"Thanks, guys. I appreciate the good news."

Xavier walked the men out and stood talking to Rainy for a moment before the phone rang again. It was almost time for Ken to arrive, so he poured himself yet another mug of coffee and picked up the last pastry. A few minutes later, Ken popped into his office and made himself at home.

"Rainy's pastry tray is empty. You must have had company."

"I did, but I also just finished my third one. It's been a tough few days. What's the bad news from you today?"

Sipping the hot coffee, Ken sat down in a large chair in front of the desk and stretched his long legs out. "The Stringer Group is still arguing about the contract. After talking to the president of the group, I got no satisfaction with his answers. So I went directly to their lawyer. I had to demand his name, as they didn't want to get their attorney involved. That should tell you something right there. The stockholders are miffed at the president of the company, as you know, and I'm betting someone won't be holding his seat much longer."

"So what did their lawyer say?"

"I sent him the copy of the contract, and highlighted the paragraph where it says either party can break the contract within ninety days. You know, the standard blah, blah, blah."

"Considering it was only about three weeks before the shareholders began to squawk, there shouldn't be an issue. Besides, since they are unhappy with the contract anyway, I would think they would be the ones to cancel the project instead. Why aren't they?"

"The president is trying to keep the contract as is because he thinks they are out of line with their demands. Are they?"

"I think so, or I wouldn't have agreed to the original terms. That's why I want out."

"I assumed as much, and their lawyer and I are in agreement that they have no case."

"You will finish handling things and I won't have to hear their name again?"

Ken chuckled. "Yeah. I got things handled. Their lawyer will send a signed agreement to that fact by next week. If I don't get it, I will personally fly out there and get it myself."

"Sure. You just want to get out of the office again."

"Something like that."

"What else is new? How's Gary?"

"Nothing new. Gary is on vacation taking his lovely family somewhere fun while I slave away in the office doing all his work."

"You love it and you know it."

"I know, I know. Besides. I'll be taking a week or so myself when he gets back."

"Figured as much." Xavier paused and then said, "I might sell the company."

Ken sat up straight, and practically fell off the chair. "What? Are you kidding me?"

He shook his head. "I came to the realization about the possibility this morning while talking to the auditors."

"The books are okay?"

"Oh, sure. But I have had a lot of changes lately, and I came to the realization last night that I was sick of traveling."

"Wow. I never thought I'd see the day you would consider selling out."

"Me neither, actually. Until this last year, I figured I'd be doing this till I died. When I look back on the projects I turned down, I believe that some of them would have been fine to take on. But I don't think I have the heart to do all the work anymore. I've done a lot of self-reflection in the last several hours."

Ken sat back again and relaxed. "It sounds like it. You still have that new project in Churchtown, right?"

"Yes. It's just getting started. Pete needed to retire because his wife is sick, and Jimmy isn't coming back. He found himself a girl in St. Louis and is staying there. We will send someone down to check on the crew and see how many are returning. Dave's bunch is already in Churchtown. Maybe it's time to quit. My guys are stretched too thin to take anything else on. The Churchtown project is huge and will take a couple of years to complete. And even Stormy is leaving town."

"Stormy is jumping ship too? Are you scaring everyone away?"

"I must be. If Rainy quits I'm in a heap of trouble." Ken laughed, and then got up for more coffee. About that time Rainy brought in a few more pastries.

"You're darn right you'll be in trouble if I quit. Ken, I thought you might need a little treat. Sorry I couldn't get in here sooner, but duty calls."

"Thanks, Rainy. Your pig of a boss inhaled the ones you had in here previously."

"I know. That's nothing new. You'll like these. There is a new shop across the street and they are to die for."

Ken took a bite. "Mm, mm. You're right," he said, his mouth full. Rainy laughed on her way out the door. Ken looked over at Xavier. "It's no wonder you had three of these this morning. I'll stop by their shop and pick some up for my office."

Xavier's mouth drooled as he looked at the plate of goodies but refrained from ruining his lunch. His mood had lightened since he thought about selling the company. "Anyway, back to selling. When the auditors were here, one of them mentioned he knew someone in South Dakota who might be interested in buying me out."

"That would be convenient. You wouldn't even need to have a realtor involved."

"I know. And when you try to sell a business, people automatically think you are in financial trouble, so I'd like to keep it confidential."

"I'll do whatever you need me to do to get the paperwork done on your end. Just let me know your decision."

"I will. I figure this could be a long process, so I'm not getting my hopes up. Winter is coming quickly, and everything slows down then. I'll have more time to myself, not having to fly all over the country." He paused. "I'm not sure selling my business is what I need to do. Maybe sell the properties and dissolve the company. What do you think?"

While Xavier was talking, Ken was gobbling up

another pastry. "I will investigate the best way to sell or dissolve the company. By dissolving it, you won't have your name associated with any of your old properties any longer." He shrugged. "I'll figure it out. In the meantime, I better go across the street and get a box of these treats, then get back to the office. Yummy." He picked up another one, emptied the coffeepot into his travel mug, and left the office, thanking Rainy for the pastries on the way out.

Rainy popped into the office. "I'm going to go down to the sub shop. Want your usual for lunch?"

"Sure thing." Rainy turned to leave the office. "Wait. I have a question for you. Have a seat."

"What's up?"

"Can we get by for the rest of the year without replacing Stormy?"

Rainy frowned. "I suppose I could do some of it. I used to a long time ago. She could show me the ropes again. Why?"

"I'm thinking of making a few changes, and right now, I don't want to take on any new employees if possible. We are always needing to add or subtract off the crews, but I don't want to hire anybody new right now."

"You sure the audit went well?"

"Of course. That's not it. I've done a lot of thinking lately, and I need to make a few changes. I'll let you know when I formulate a plan. You know I depend on you for everything, so I won't let you wonder too much longer. I kicked around a few ideas this morning, and the more I think about them, the more I like where I am going with it."

"Xavier, I know you depend on me, and I appreciate everything you have done for me over the years. And Stormy too. Whatever you need or do, I'll support your decision."

"Thanks. You're the best."

"I know. I'm still waiting for that big bonus check. The kid left for college last week and I have big bills to pay."

Xavier shook his head and laughed. "Christmas, my dear. Bonus at Christmas, just like always."

Rainy chuckled on her way out the door to answer the phone. "I know. A girl can always try, though."

Lunch rolled around, and Xavier worked while eating. He answered emails and texts, kept in touch with Buck, and Dave shot him a reply that things were going well. Rainy contacted Alan, who was happy as a clam to be able to head to Missouri for a task. He rarely worked these days but stayed on the payroll "just in case" Xavier needed him. He always paid Alan a hefty salary for the jobs he sent him out on, knowing that he and his wife could use the extra money. That would be one more person who would be out of a job if he sold out. Sighing again, he sat back when he realized he had been doing that a lot all day. He wasn't a sigher by nature, but life had a way of throwing curve balls.

Rainy left for the day, and Xavier sat in his office for a few moments before sneaking up the back way to his apartment. There wasn't any food in his refrigerator or cupboard, so he was going to have to go out to eat. Still not wanting to run into the usual crowd, he picked up food at a drive-thru and returned home. The evenings were becoming chilly, so he wouldn't be sitting on the small patio and watching the sunset. He hunkered down in front of the television and attempted to find a movie to watch. He turned in early, not having slept well the evening before. He could work through his thoughts tomorrow. That would be soon enough.

12

Leaving off a conversation with "we need to talk" is always a bad sign. Charity knew she probably shouldn't have said it, but when Xavier cancelled on her once again, it was the last straw. She wasn't going to stop living while waiting on him. She was just getting her life back on track after moving home. No, it was time to quit looking back and go forward. They had blown their chance at a relationship more than once, and maybe it was time to give up permanently.

The stained glass pieces turned out better each time she made one, and she realized that they were good enough to sell. Originally, feeling selfish, she didn't want them placed in the homes around her. She felt that her pieces were only hers to enjoy. But after working with new colors, designs, and ideas, Charity secretly made a few for the front doors of the homes on her side of the block. They all faced the sun and would be a great addition. Figuring out a price was the hard part. Charity called Mr. Piedmont, and he stopped over one day to inspect the most recent projects. He immediately set a price on them and took some back to the gallery to sell. The ones she made for the doors were much smaller, and she hid them from Mr. Piedmont. But now Charity knew what price to ask if Buck would agree to install them in the transoms of the rehabbed homes. If not, she knew Mr. Piedmont would take them.

Previously, Mr. Piedmont and his helpers hung

Charity's paintings as a collage on her large open wall. He agreed most of them were not good enough to sell at the gallery but did look at her painting in progress. While checking out the stained glass, he looked over her painting once again and stated it was coming along nicely. But the verdict was still out, and she could count on him to be honest. Charity had many long, empty days and evenings to work on the painting, but she took her time and didn't rush. Her changing moods affected the way the painting was coming along, and, now that she was mad at Xavier, she hadn't touched it in a week. Instead, she went to see Georgia or went out with friends. She invited Martine over occasionally for an evening on the patio. All in all, she was trying to stay busy with life outside her home. After five years hiding out, it was an effort, but she felt better after she visited with the outside world.

Buck stopped by when Charity teased him with the thought of getting his hands on some stained glass. Unsurprisingly, Martine was tagging along. They looked at her first two samples, and both thought they were beautiful. Charity admitted she had gone over and measured the transoms to make sure of the size, just in case Xavier agreed to pay the hefty price for the product. Buck took a few pictures and sent them off to Rainy. Rainy, in turn, showed them to Xavier, who instantly agreed to the price. They would have to take the expense into account when they sold the homes, though. The two homes that were already under contract had not been locked into a final price yet, since the families contracted for them while still unfinished. Xavier's plan was to keep all the remodels the same price on both sides of the street, so getting that initial price right was imperative. He didn't want the neighbors comparing notes wondering why one home was more expensive than the other.

With the go-ahead to finish more pieces, the three of them walked across the street and took more measurements. By the time they were done, they decided to go to supper. Charity stopped to get a jacket, then they took off. By the time she was back home, another day was finished without any messages from Xavier. Disappointed, yet relieved, Charity called it a night.

Martine knew that Charity was upset with Xavier and hadn't seen him for quite some time. Buck didn't know what was going on, and he wasn't about to ask Xavier. He and Martine were getting along very well, and that was all that mattered. His boss was on his own.

Four days later, Xavier felt like he could get away from the office and head to Churchtown again. Several issues were resolved in those few days, including getting out of that crazy contract. Relieved he could put that behind him, all he had to do was let Alan do his job in Missouri and keep an eye on the Churchtown project. The Florida construction was completed and his property manager for the condos seemed to be doing a great job. He thought about flying down to see his parents, but they were going to leave on a cruise in the next couple of weeks. He was happy they were living a good life, and hoped he could say the same for himself one day.

Closing the apartment, he stopped by the pastry shop, then headed back to Churchtown. Rainy wasn't even in the office before he took off that morning, so Xavier left a note on her desk. On the drive back to his house, it felt like he was coming home. Maybe that was how Charity felt when she returned to her loft. Smiling, he was counting on finding her home when he arrived. And he hoped a box of delicious pastries would help smooth out her anger at him. She had every right to be mad. He had been terrible lately, breaking dates and leaving town without notice. It wasn't any more fair to her than when she did the same to him years ago. Although not quite the same thing, when he looked back, it was very similar to how he felt. They apologized to each other for the past, but he needed to apologize for the here and now.

Pulling up in front of Charity's home, he picked up the box of pastries and crossed his fingers. Knocking, he waited for a few minutes before knocking a little louder. He finally heard someone yell and became very nervous. Charity opened the door, and her mouth dropped open.

"Xavier. I didn't know you were coming. I was expecting a delivery."

"Will these do instead?"

Charity looked at the box in his hands. "Donuts?"

"There is a variety of pastries. I assure you, they are all delicious."

She shook her head. "Where are my manners? Come on in. I was in the back working and didn't hear you."

Xavier came across the threshold and closed the door behind him. Maybe the donuts helped, after all. "I'm sorry I didn't call first. I left Oakville bright and early so I could get these here while they were still fresh."

"Come on up to the apartment. Let's see what you have. There should be enough coffee left from this morning." He followed her upstairs and set the box on the table. "Yip. Enough to pour a couple more cups. Do you want one?"

"Sure. I think I gained ten pounds once I found out that the new pastry shop was across the street from my office."

Charity popped open the lid. "Ooh. These look great. Let's see." She picked out a jelly-filled donut and sat down with her coffee.

Xavier joined her and chose a glazed donut. "Anything you choose will taste great."

Charity moaned in obvious delight over her choice. Taking a sip of coffee, she replied, "If a simple jelly donut is this good, I can't wait to try one of the other pastries."

"Help yourself. I had one on the way. They are irresistible."

Just as he was going to apologize, Charity heard someone knocking. "Excuse me. That will be my delivery."

A few minutes later, she returned and picked out another donut before sitting back down. The couple ate their fill before Xavier approached the elephant in the room. After all, it was his fault there was one there to begin with. Charity was being selfless again, allowing them a moment of time without yelling at him, because he knew she wanted to. Again, he was thankful for the pastry box in front of him. He finally dove in.

"I'm sorry for the past couple of months. Me running all over the countryside was rude and I should have been putting you first." He held up his hand when she attempted to say something in response. "I've been doing a lot of soul searching lately. I had an epiphany of sorts when I arrived at my apartment in Oakville. I walked in and realized how much I hated traveling. All I've done for years is zip around the country making deals, buying and selling property. Even before you came home, I was becoming disillusioned with my work. This project is the last deal I've made in over a year. That is so unlike me. I'm usually rocking a deal every few months. I own property all over the States, and keeping track of it all is wearing on me. It's a good thing I have great employees like Rainy and Buck." He paused and tried to decide if he wanted another pastry or not. He shook his head and closed the box.

Charity took the silence as a moment to respond if she so chose. Still, no one spoke for a moment. Licking the sugar from her fingers, she finally had to ask, "What are you going to do about it?"

"Believe it or not, I think I'm going to try and sell the company." Charity gasped. "Well, not the company per se, but most of my property. I need to keep the company intact because I will be keeping this project and the condos I have in Florida. Everything else can go."

"Seriously? I can't imagine you not working eighty hours a week any longer."

"It may take a very long time to sell all my property off, but I will be keeping some because I need to have some type of income. Of course, the company will still sell these homes, which will fund the beginning of the apartment buildings here. Then I will keep them as an investment. That's my plan, anyway. But I have to find someone to buy all the rest of my property."

"How do you do that?"

"I'm not sure yet. There is a lead, but I probably won't hear from anyone for some time. I don't want to mention or broadcast it, because it could ruin a company. People think you're going bankrupt or something instead of just wanting out."

"I can see that. I won't mention it to anyone."

"If this lead doesn't work out, I will begin to list the properties at their locations and work on selling them individually. But it'll take some big operators to buy some of my investments. I worked long and hard to rehab many of the buildings I own. I won't be giving them away."

"So, in the meantime?"

"I'm here. I'm home. I will probably have to run to Oakville occasionally, but you could go with me. I mean, if you want to. Rainy and I talked the day before I left. She knows I'm done investing. That way, if a call comes in, she can say I'm not interested at this time due to the extensive project I'm working on. That is the truth, by the way. Not that I'm needed here, necessarily, but you are here, and I'd like to work on our relationship. Of course, we haven't really built one yet, but I'd like to try again. The past keeps creeping up, and I'd like to put it behind us, where it belongs."

"I'd like that, Xavier. I really would. Are you serious about staying around?"

"I bought a house to live in. In the back of my mind, I was evidently thinking long-term, but didn't realize that I meant for years. Funny. Coming back to where I grew up after all these years seems right, though."

"Yes, it does." Charity got up and went to sit on Xavier's lap. "If you promise to stay, I'd love to build a life with you."

"It's a deal." They passionately kissed for a moment. Xavier looked up at her and smiled. "Now. How about another donut?"

She laughed, slapped him on a shoulder, and got up to make another pot of coffee. "How about I fix a healthy lunch first?"

"Spoilsport. I suppose that would be okay."

Xavier had a pouty look on his face, and Charity couldn't help but laugh. She pulled some sandwich makings out of the refrigerator and put it all on the table in front of him. "Here. Put together whatever you want on your sandwich. I'll get our coffee mugs refilled."

The couple talked throughout lunch and dessert. They had much to discuss and tried to stay away from the past.

Charity talked about her stained glass and how she'd picked up her paintbrush once again. Later, they went to the studio to check out the painting. She knew that she could get back to work on it now that her life was no longer off-kilter. Xavier was meant to be in her life. She knew that, and now he also knew that to be a fact. He was impressed with the painting, but she knew there were a few mistakes she needed to take care of before moving on. Charity didn't bother pointing them out, as she knew they were only obvious to her. The few hours they spent together passed quickly, but Xavier needed to go home and touch base with Buck and let him know what was in the works. They promised to get together the following day and would set something up later. Buck was at the house when Xavier arrived. He went downstairs to catch him up on what was going to happen with the company.

Xavier explained how things changed dramatically in the last few days. "Listen. I know that leaves you high and dry in a couple of years, but I promise that you will be taken care of. You have certainly earned a huge bonus for all the years I've leaned on you. I need to talk to my accountants once we have a bead on how quickly this will happen, but I want to be sure to give you a share of my profits in the long term."

Buck looked perplexed. "What do you mean?"

"You and Rainy are the most important people in my organization. I want to form some type of partnership that includes you two once I get all the excess property sold. There will be long-term income from the Florida housing, plus the apartment houses here. We have to place a value on all of that, plus figure out how much actual income we will get. Some years will be better than others, I'm sure. But I need to take care of you guys. Rainy can continue to run the office, but she won't have to be there as much. If you want to work, you can act as the property manager here instead of hiring someone. I have a feeling you are pretty serious about Martine."

"Yes, I'm very serious about Martine. We haven't known each other that long, but I honestly think I'll ask her to marry me. I'd like her to meet my family too. I've met her mother already. And, believe it or not, I told her a long time ago that I'd quit my job to stay with her, so being the property manager sounds just fine to me. I'm not sure I understand the partnership idea you mentioned, though. You mean, Rainy and I would receive actual income from the business?"

"Yes. I would like to make the three of us equal partners. Ken will be happy to make sure everything is legal, but I need to get out from under a passel of property first. And we need to finish this project. In the meantime, I'll continue to pay you two your usual wages and bonuses. I mean, if that's all right with you."

"And Rainy agreed?"

"Wholeheartedly. In fact, she figures that's the only way she will get her big bonus she always harps on me about." Buck laughed so hard he almost fell off his chair. Xavier joined him, and the laughter felt good. He had been under so much stress in the last year.

When Buck wiped his eyes, he asked, "And what about Charity?"

Xavier smiled. "We're good. In fact, better than good. A box of pastries can fix anything."

"What?" Buck scrunched up his face in confusion.

He chuckled. "Let's just say, I apologized and think we are on the right track. Finally."

"Great. Martine and I have been rooting for you two."

"Maybe the four of us could do something this weekend."

"Wonderful."

"And don't talk about me selling my property to anyone. I don't need the crew to get uncomfortable. I need them to stick this project out."

"That reminds me. Dave is thinking about going out on his own."

"Really? That would actually be a good thing. He can take the crew with him when he's done here. He won't leave until this job is over, will he?"

"No. He knows where his bread is buttered, but he is also saving every penny he has to open his own business back in Oakville when this job is over."

"Nice. I think this is playing out quite well. I forgot to tell you that Jimmy is staying in St. Louis and Alan is going down to see how much of the crew will be sticking with us."

"Huh. Things are kind of falling into place, then, aren't they?"

"Yeah. Now, if I can just get the ball rolling to make it

all happen."

"You will." Xavier got up to leave. "And by the way, welcome home. It will be good to have you around more."

"You'll probably get sick of me now. But with Charity and Martine to keep us otherwise occupied, we should be good to go."

"That's what I'm saying." Buck walked over and gave Xavier a man-hug, then backed away. "See you later, boss."

Two weeks later, Xavier received an email about his properties from the company in South Dakota. They were seriously interested in several of his holdings, but not all of them. It was a start, and he responded that he would be happy to have Zoom calls to hold preliminary talks. Then they would have their team go look at the properties and have them evaluated. It was going to be a long process, but now that Xavier had made a life-changing decision, he wasn't too worried about the time frame. He just wanted it all done correctly.

The holidays were upon them, and the weather turned snowy and cold. The crews completed as much work as possible on the outside of each building so they could spend the winter working inside. Dave did a great job scheduling the workflow, and now they were spending the cold months finishing several homes. The first two homes next to Charity's were now sold and the families had moved in. After the first of the year, it looked like the last two on that side of the block would be sold also. The crew continued to work on two homes at a time, scheduling the subcontractors right behind them. By spring, Dave planned to start on the second block, barring complications along the way.

Xavier always gave his employees two weeks off during the Christmas holidays. It was a good time for everyone to take a break and get recharged. Even the office was closed. This year, Buck was taking Martine home to his family, and Xavier was taking Charity to his parents' place in Florida. His sister and her family would be there also, so the condo would be filled to the brim. There were enough bedrooms between the two for them all to stay, which was nice.

Buck and Xavier went Christmas shopping together. The jewelry store was across town and away from prying eyes. They picked out their favorite rings, hoping the girls liked them. Buck asked for a setting that might represent Martine's heritage. They scoured the store until Buck was satisfied with a fine band of eagle feathers, and the jeweler would add the stones to another band, similar in style, to go with it. Xavier wanted something simple but dressy. Charity was a shiny bauble type, but he didn't want gaudy. He figured he spent way too much, yet the simple but fancy set looked perfect to him. The store clerk reassured them their girlfriends could return after the holidays to make any adjustments needed. And if they didn't like what the men picked out, they could return them and get something else. After the dollar amount the two dropped in the store, the jewelers certainly wanted happy customers. The two went back a few days later to pick up their sets. Now all they had to do was find the right moment to pop the question.

The time leading up to the holidays was busy for both Martine and Charity. They were invited to several events, and the two often attended together. The men begged off several times, and Charity didn't seem to mind these days. After all, he was staying close to home. She hadn't heard much else about Xavier selling out, but figured he would tell her if something came up. She was becoming anxious about meeting his family and spending several days in Florida. She was glad to be staying in his parents' house, and not with his sister's family. She wasn't sure she was ready for the busyness of a big family while trying to relax.

Martine finished her special orders for the year and was enjoying the stress-free moments. Cleaning her workshop was time-consuming. She hadn't done a thorough cleaning since she moved in six years ago. After taking care of the buildup of trash, she looked around and decided to give the walls a coat of paint. With no obstructions, it would be a simple job. Remembering that Charity rented scaffolding, she decided that would be a great solution. Charity offered to pay for the paint and scaffolding when Martine called to find out where to get the equipment. After all, it was still her building. While high in the air, she cleaned the ceiling of cobwebs and dirt. That also meant another sweeping of the floor. Before long, Martine was throwing a quick coat of paint on the walls.

Choosing a bright white color to help lighten the area, Martine studied her lighting and decided to put in new fixtures. She asked Buck to look at the area now that it was painted and told him what she wanted to do about the lighting. He made some suggestions but also offered to have one of the electricians come by and handle the installation once she bought the new lights. He reassured her it would be no big deal, since she had the scaffolding in place and the building didn't need new wiring. She finally agreed.

Just before the crews took their Christmas break, Buck had one of the electricians come over to install the lights for Martine. Between the old system and new, there would be enough lighting so she wouldn't have any shadows in the room. Buck was right. It only took the man a couple of hours to install the new system, and she made sure the lights were aiming correctly toward her work area. Martine was thrilled with the changes and knew she would enjoy the new lights when she went back to work after the first of the year.

And then, suddenly, the neighborhood quieted down. The work crews left, the traffic lessened on the highway out front, and the snow began to fall. Christmas was right around the corner. Charity and Xavier headed to Florida, and Buck and Martine drove to Oakville to spend a few days with his family. They would return to spend some time with her mother later. Buck was going to wait until they were at her mother's to ask Martine to marry him. Xavier planned to take Charity for a ride in the golf cart to some botanical gardens not far from the condos. There, he planned to find a quiet little corner and propose. Although Charity had met his parents years ago, he knew she was still anxious about staying at their place. His sister hadn't been around much when they were dating, so there would be a whole group of strangers for the holiday meal. He promised Charity they could fly home early if she became overwhelmed by the noise.

A few days later, Buck was visiting with Martine's mother in the living room. Martine brought in a tray of drinks and an afternoon snack and set it on the coffee table. Sitting down beside Buck, he reached over and patted her leg before bending over and looking under the coffee table.

"What are you looking at?"

"I don't know. Something doesn't look quite right." He got off the couch and knelt to look under the coffee table. Reaching his hand behind one of the legs. "Hmm. What is this?" He pulled out the ring box and turned around. While still kneeling, and opening the box at the same time, he said, "Will you marry me?"

Martine's mouth dropped open in shock. Finally, she reached out to grab Buck by the neck. "Yes. Yes. Yes. I will marry you." Buck put the ring on her finger, and she gasped at the intricate design. "This is beautiful. Oh, Buck. I love you so much."

Buck managed to get up beside Martine even though she was strangling him. "I love you too."

Martine's mother was teary-eyed and hugged her

daughter. She was also impressed with the eagle feathers on the bands, and thought Buck was very thoughtful to think of Martine's heritage. She only wished her husband were still alive to see his little girl moving on to the next stage of her life. It was a beautiful day.

Xavier had to wait an extra day to take Charity for the ride he originally planned for the day after Christmas. The rain wouldn't stop, and he wanted to ask her before they went back home. Thankfully, they finally woke up to sunny skies, so he rushed her out the door before the weather decided to change its mind. The garden was only a few blocks away, and they were soon walking through the beautiful flowers. The rain brought out the fresh blooms, and everything sparkled from the dew still on the leaves. Xavier knew there was a bench not too far in and made his way there. They sat and talked, and he mentioned needing to retie one of his shoes.

"I guess while I'm down here I'll retie the other one too."

"You might as well. It seems like if one comes undone, the other soon follows."

"The bushes across the way with the red blooms are gorgeous."

Charity looked over and smiled. "Yes, they are."

Xavier got into position and knelt before Charity. "You are gorgeous too. Will you marry me?" He held up the ring.

A gardener happened to be walking by at that time and yelled out, "Say yes!"

Charity slapped her hands against both sides of her

face in awe, then dropped her eyes from the ring to Xavier's face. "Yes. I will marry you." Xavier stood up, pulling Charity with him. They kissed and hugged, then he twirled her around. "To our future." Then he kissed her senseless.

Eventually, they continued their walk through the gardens, stopping occasionally for a quick kiss. Xavier warned her that the house was going to be mass of confusion and noise when they returned. He hadn't told any of his family ahead of time, trying to keep the proposal a secret, just in case she said no. And he wasn't kidding. Everyone hollered and wanted a hug. Sometimes several hugs. The children went crazy with excitement, just because the adults did. Xavier was right. It was a little overwhelming at times. But Charity figured if she could handle gallery events, she could handle this too. Besides, she loved them all.

Life settled into a routine after the first of the year. It didn't take long for the construction crews to get back to work. Charity was done picking and choosing colors for the buildings in a two-block area. She even had the colors chosen for the homes that were to be built on the empty lots. Now she was concentrating on finishing up the last of the stained glass. Only the homes on her block were going to have them installed to set them apart from the next block. The color choices were different, also. A little bolder, but not garish. It was a fine line to walk, but Charity thought the two blocks would look like a neighborhood, yet be separate.

Martine and Charity giggled and laughed like a couple of schoolgirls once they got together after the holidays. They shared their engagement stories and discussed where and when they wanted to get married. Xavier couldn't see any reason to wait. They had put marriage off for years. Charity couldn't help but agree, and they decided on a simple wedding in front of a judge in a couple of months. Martine and Buck planned a standard church wedding in the fall, and hoped to integrate some of her father's heritage in with the ceremony. It was going to take some planning, but her mother was ecstatic to make it happen. After all, her little girl was getting married.

Xavier kept to his promise, and anytime he needed to go to Oakville, he invited Charity. Sometimes she went with him, and sometimes not, but was given the choice. They were in a good place in their relationship, and they both wanted to hold strong and continue to build upon the new foundation they had set.

It was mid-January before Xavier heard from the firm that was interested in buying his properties. They had already been out across the States looking at each one, and Xavier's auditors gave them the financial information they needed. After a special meeting with their board, the group chose several of the properties, and a bid would be forthcoming. Xavier did not set a price ahead of time, but had the property evaluations in hand. He wasn't going to play hardball. If the two of them came to a fair price after a little back and forth, he would be happy to let them all go. In the meantime, he called a realtor in the location of the ones that the firm weren't interested in, and put them on the market. He hoped he'd have a solid answer from the firm before getting married.

Xavier also needed Ken to finish putting the details on the new business contracts, with Rainy and Buck as co-owners. Ken tried to convince Xavier that he still needed controlling interest, but even if his shares were larger, Buck and Rainy could still outvote him if they wanted. At this point in time, the company was just a matter of investments with no more buying. Ken got busy and formed a new LLC, then planned to dissolve the current company when the last property was sold. That would mean a clean break from the old company, and Xavier would be out from under the behemoth. The two condos that Xavier owned for his family in Florida would be transferred out of the company and into his and Charity's names. The rest of the property, along with the Churchtown project, would be settled into a new LLC called *Looking Forward*.

The biggest surprise of the moment was when Rainy called Xavier after the New Year and told him that she and her longtime companion had eloped to Hawaii for the holidays. Her son and his daughter went with them, and their blended family had a great time. Even after all their years together, both had sworn they would never get married again. But with the children now in college and making their own way in the world, somehow, the two decided it was time to make it legal.

For a wedding date, Charity picked the first day of spring. She chose the day so they could always remember to look forward to the weather changing seasons. Besides, she felt like Xavier would find the date easier to remember, and he pretended to be offended at the thought of him forgetting something as important as their wedding date. Martine and Buck stood up for them during the service, and, within a few minutes, they were man and wife. Georgia, Gary, Maurice, and Mr. Piedmont were at the service too. The couple rented a large room for the reception and invited the whole crew to the restaurant for a buffet supper to celebrate. Rainy and her new husband arrived too. The party went long into the night, even though it was a Tuesday. The new couple settled into Xavier's house, and Buck moved into Charity's loft. The basement at the house would soon become her new studio.

Buck and Martine were trying to decide whether or not to buy a home somewhere but hated giving up the workshop. It was perfect to make her large sculptures, and she had just completed the upgrades. Charity came to the rescue and offered to sell them the home. That was all well and good, but if the couple had children there wouldn't be any extra bedrooms. Xavier gave it some thought and found a solution. Or so he hoped.

"I think I have solved the housing problem." The four of them were sitting in the living room of Charity's former home. "These two buildings are fairly close together, right?" Everyone nodded. "Why don't we connect the two? We can tear open the two walls where the old stores were, and build across. Then, toward the back, we can make a walled-in garden space, patio, or lawn. Whatever you want. It can be fenced in, so if you do have children then they have a place to play without getting out in the traffic."

Charity smiled, having agreed with the plan before they left home. "Here is a sketch I drew up while Xavier was telling me about it this morning." She handed it over. "The addition won't even affect the roofline. The new roof can be tied right in."

Buck looked at the drawing, then back at his boss. "So I would buy both properties, and we would add a connector between the two? That would be where I would make bedrooms."

Xavier shrugged his shoulders. "Or one of the living rooms can be made into bedrooms. However you want it. We have the building crews here, so there isn't an issue with getting someone to put it together. Once you have the plans made up, they can move in and take care of the whole thing. Of course, you need to get a permit to do all of that. But you get along well with everyone at the city level, so it shouldn't be a problem, and it's not like you don't have access to an architect."

Martine was mulling it all over. "Buck, I'd hate to give up my workshop. Since you are going to be the property manager eventually, living here only makes sense. I say we try to make this work. After all, I always wanted a big house."

He nodded. "We'll give this some thought, and I'll talk to the architects before we make any decisions. It's important that Martine keeps her workshop, and I don't blame her. Finding a house with that kind of room is unheard of around here."

Charity nodded. "You let me know. We can stick to the same evaluation as the ones you rehabbed, right?"

"Probably."

Xavier's stomach growled and grumbled. He frowned. "Now that we have that out of the way and have solved all the problems of the world, how about we head out to supper? I'm starved." Laughing, everyone agreed.

13

ONE YEAR LATER

The neighborhoods looked completely different than they did a couple of years previous. With all the new high-end siding and beautiful colors, the homes were a hot item. The real estate agent was selling them faster than they were finished. The empty lots would eventually hold new homes that would be as similar as possible to the style of the old neighborhood. The architects did a great job with the plans.

In the meantime, the area where the apartment house was going to be built was being prepared, along with the infrastructure. What was left of the crew in Missouri returned, and they would have a steady job for at least another year or more. Dave promoted one of his men to help him manage the crews, to make his life much easier. He hadn't realized how much he would miss Pete. He was glad, though, that Pete's wife was in remission now.

Charity's old buildings were purchased by Buck, and the new plans to build between the two had gone through. It took some time because they had to join lots and then get permits to tie in the two structures. The architects improved Xavier's plan and managed to add four bedrooms. Charity's old workshop was being made into a garage with a game room built into the loft area. Martine didn't need to make any further improvements to her work area, but when they had children, Buck would put a good lock on the door to keep it safe from prying hands.

The old apartment in Xavier's house was refitted for Charity's workshop. She didn't need nearly as much space as Martine and was grateful for all the appliances and a bathroom. She could throw a load of dirty rags into the washer and keep snacks and drinks close by. Out of the way from their living quarters, she could leave a mess if she so desired. There would be no one to bother anything. Sometimes, Xavier would come down to be in the same room. He would sit on the couch and work on his computer or wear headphones and watch a movie. He was fascinated with Charity's work and watched her frequently as she formed pieces of stained glass to fit perfectly together. And the painting she had just completed was so impressive, he was afraid to get anywhere close to it in fear he would knock it over or something. Mr. Piedmont planned to stop by in the next couple of days to decide if it was worthy of hanging at the gallery. Xavier almost hoped not. He wanted it hanging in the living room instead. Most of Charity's old paintings were removed from her old place after Buck bought it. He tried to get her to leave them on the wall, but the contractors would be making a mess, and they would be in the way eventually. Buck finally agreed and took them all down. Xavier and Buck stored them safely in the basement of the house.

Charity sat back and stretched. Her swollen abdomen was getting larger all the time and made bending over her worktable difficult. She and Xavier knew they had one chance for a child. She was getting to an age when it would no longer be safe if they waited much longer. The baby was growing by leaps and bounds, and she could hardly wait to introduce the child to her daddy. Xavier got up, walked over to Charity, and gave her a big hug.

"Ready to call it a day?"

"Yes. I finished this one, and that's it. Mr. Piedmont won't go away empty-handed if he doesn't take the painting. But I won't have time to mess with any more projects for a long time."

"Do you think you will miss creating new art?"

"No." She smiled and looked into her husband's face. "I went almost six years without doing a thing. I think I can handle a little time off again. Especially if it means taking care of our little one."

He kissed her, then led her upstairs. Shutting off the light, he closed the door behind him, knowing they were starting on a new path once again. Their future looked bright. Looking forward, he knew they were right where they were supposed to be.

About The Author

Diane Winters is from Southwest Nebraska and is an avid reader of all genres. She came from a large family and grew up in a farming community. She was blessed with two children and has four grandchildren of her own. Diane has been a nurse for many years and held various positions in the healthcare field over time.

Diane appreciates the sunsets, rainstorms and rainbows, and views from the mountain tops. She and her husband enjoy traveling, and the drive time gives Diane the opportunity to work out new storylines.

You may wish to keep a watch for her next book release on her Facebook page:

www.facebook.com/ Diane L Winters